THE GREAT SUGAR WAR

THE GREAT SUGAR WAR

Written By Benjamin Ellefson

Illustrated By Kevin Cannon

Illustrated by Kevin Cannon
ISBN 13: 978-1-59298-632-3
Library of Congress Catalog Number: 2016919608
Printed in the United States of America
First Printing: 2017
21 20 19 18 17   5 4 3 2 1
Book design and typesetting by Kevin Cannon.

BEAVER'S POND
PRESS

Beaver's Pond Press
7108 Ohms Lane
Edina, MN 55439–2129
(952) 829-8818
www.BeaversPondPress.com
To order, visit www.ItascaBooks.com
or call (800)-901-3480. Reseller discounts available.

For Mom and Dad, for standing by
my side through all the battles.

Table of Contents

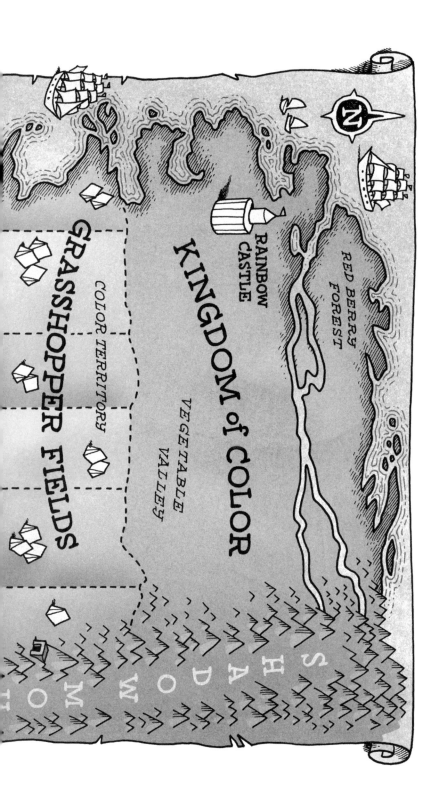

chapter 1

History Lessons

A gray squirrel darted across the green grass. Brandon gazed out the classroom window, studying the squirrel's every move. It stopped, sniffed the ground, and then sprang ahead a few more steps. Ever since learning of the adventures of Grandpa Alvin, Permy, and Ronaldo, Brandon had paid closer attention to all the squirrels and other animals he saw. He tried talking to them whenever he got close enough, but so far, none had answered him.

"Brandon! Brandon!" Miss Carter interrupted. "Brandon, will you stop daydreaming and pay attention? Pass your homework forward."

The realization that he was at school rushed back into Brandon's head. He turned his attention back to his teacher, pulled out his homework, and passed it forward. Brandon never had much interest in school. He did fairly well, but it bored him. He would rather be running through the neighborhood playing with Steven and his friends.

"Okay, class," Miss Carter announced. "Everyone take out your history books and turn to chapter thirteen."

In unison, the students sifted through their backpacks and pulled out their books. Once the class was ready, Miss Carter began.

"I hope everyone finished the reading last night. Now who can tell me the cause of the Great Grayness?"

The usual suspects in class were excited to answer. Elizabeth in the front row had her hand raised high, surely with the right answer. Michael in the second row had a confident grin as his hand wiggled in the air.

Brandon was sitting in the back of the room on the far side by the windows. He was never one to volunteer answers to the class. He had mastered the art of looking as if he were paying attention, but not enough to be called on.

But today was different. Brandon had forgotten to do his reading last night, but he still knew the answer. His hand shot straight into the air, and his face beamed with pride. Miss Carter took notice of the special occasion and called on Brandon to answer. An excited smile grew across his face as he stood.

"The Great Grayness was caused by the snakes who controlled the Color Factory," he explained. "It drained the color from the land through underground pipes. Without color in the land, the crops didn't grow, and the people were forced to eat ice cream and candy from the king. And without the color from good fruits and vegetables, the people lost their color too. But that ended when my grandpa defeated the vipers in the Color Factory and rescued the princesses."

Giggles spread throughout the classroom. Elizabeth rolled her eyes at Brandon.

Miss Carter gave Brandon a disappointed scowl and replied, "We are studying history now, Brandon, not creative writing. Please do not waste the class's time with your daydreams." She then called on Elizabeth to answer.

"The Great Grayness was caused by the goblins beyond the Shadow Mountains," Elizabeth explained. "After nine years of war, the Crimson Guards defeated the goblin king and restored the color to the land."

"But that's wrong," Brandon declared. "My grandfather was there. The goblins didn't steal the color. That was a lie told by the king."

"That's enough, Brandon," Miss Carter stated sternly. "It's bad enough to not do your homework and make up stories, but there is no excuse to speak ill of the king. Go to the office right now."

"But Miss Carter, I'm only telling the truth of what happened," Brandon replied.

"Stop it right now," Miss Carter said. "You could go to prison for saying such words. Pick up your things, and go to the office. The principal will be calling your parents."

Dejectedly, Brandon grabbed his history book and his notebook and shoved them into his backpack. He bowed his head as he walked to the classroom door.

"And pray that I decide not to report you to the royal authorities," Miss Carter threatened. "It would be a shame if this class had one less student tomorrow."

Brandon slowly inched his way down the hallway toward the principal's office. He couldn't understand why the history book was telling such lies or why Miss Carter got so angry about him telling the truth of what happened. With every footstep closer, the fear of his impending doom grew within him. The principal was a thick man with a big mustache. He was a mean man whom all the kids avoided at all costs. Rumors spread through the halls that if you were unfortunate enough to be sent to his office, you could literally see steam shoot from his ears when he yelled at you.

The thoughts of the Color Factory swirled in Brandon's head. If only he could prove he was right. Then he could avoid the wicked tongue-lashing of the principal and his parents. Just then, a spark ignited in Brandon's head. His grandfather had been there; he was the hero of the Kingdom of Color. All he needed was Grandpa Alvin to talk to Miss Carter and explain everything.

Brandon paused in the hallway. He looked behind him. No one was around. The halls were silent except for the muffled sound of the teachers talking in the classrooms.

Only one set of doors was open during the day—the main front doors. They were past the school office. He needed to take the chance.

As quietly as he could, Brandon opened the nearest locker and hid his backpack. Then he crept down the hall alongside the wall of lockers, pausing when he reached the office. As carefully as he could, he lay down on the floor and began slithering past the office.

The front of the school office was lined with full-length windows so the staff could see all the activity in the hallway. The bottom portion of the windows was tinted for decoration. Brandon hoped he could keep low enough and quiet enough to not be detected. Within a few moments, he was halfway across. He was convinced he would make it safely, but then his sneaker

squeaked loudly against the tile floor.

Brandon's heart jumped into his throat and beat a thousand times a minute. Instantly, he stopped and flattened closer to the floor. He tried to listen for someone coming to investigate the noise, but he could not hear above the sound of his heart.

After a few more moments, he had to keep going. Trying to avoid making the squeak again, he pulled himself forward with his arms. When he was past the office, he leaped to his feet and raced out the door.

As fast as his feet could take him, he ran across the school parking lot to the yard across the street. If he could make it across the street before the security guard saw him, he could sneak through the shadows of the neighborhood backyards all the way to his grandpa's house. Fortunately, luck was with him. Within a few minutes of running at top speed, he was at Grandpa Alvin's house.

Ding! Ding! Ding! Brandon pushed on the doorbell as fast as he could, but there was no answer. He was too excited and didn't want to be seen outside of school during the day, so he raced to his grandfather's vegetable garden in the front yard. Under a small statue of a squirrel was the hidden key. He grabbed it and let himself into the house.

"Grandpa! Grandpa Alvin! It's me, Brandon!" he yelled.

There was still no answer. It took only a few minutes to search through the entire house. It was empty.

Brandon began to be worried. His grandfather was always home. Brandon had no idea where Grandpa Alvin might ever go. He sat down on his grandpa's old couch, a million thoughts dancing in his head. What would he do now? The school must have known by now that he was gone. They were probably looking for him. Where was his grandfather? When would he be back? Would his Grandpa Alvin be back before someone else found him? How could he clear his name and prove his story was true?

"Proof!" Brandon said out loud. That was it. Maybe his grandfather had proof. Maybe he had a medal or a ribbon or a certificate or something.

Brandon first looked in his grandfather's bedroom. He riffled through the dresser drawers, but all he found were clothes. Next he went to the closet, but all he saw were shirts and shoes. Then he saw a shoe box lying on the corner of the floor next to his grandfather's shotgun, but a peek inside only revealed shells for the gun.

Brandon then looked in his grandfather's office. He searched through some papers on the desk and in the drawers. They all looked like bills or other grown-up garbage.

As he was flipping through the folders in the file cabinet, he noticed there was an odd space in the back. He pulled the drawer out all the way and noticed a thin box hidden in the back. Carefully, he pulled it out, set it on the desk, and opened it. Inside was a folded paper that looked very old. Gently, Brandon unfolded it and discovered a map of the Kingdom of Color. But this was not the map he was used to looking at in school. Smack in the middle of the map was the Color Factory.

A smile grew across Brandon's face. This map was proof that the Color Factory existed. He could now be vindicated from his teacher's accusations. Excited, he started back to school with his salvation in his hand. But before he reached the front door, Brandon realized something. This map was hand drawn. There was no way his teacher would accept it as official proof.

Brandon needed something more concrete. He needed to find the Color Factory himself. And with this map, he could do it.

chapter 2

Escape to the Color Factory

Brandon was ready to set off on his journey. He had the map to the Color Factory in his left pocket and his trusty pocketknife in his right. When he opened the front door to exit, he saw Officer Reed standing right in front of him.

Dressed in a black uniform with a golden badge on his chest, Officer Reed was the school's security guard. He was responsible for making sure every student attended every class to learn what was required. Most of the students hated him and pronounced his name "Re-Ed" to make fun of him, but they knew he was not someone to mess with.

Before Brandon could move, Officer Reed grabbed him by the shoulder. "There you are, little boy," he said with wicked smile. "You have some learning to do."

Brandon struggled, but he was no match for the officer's strong grip. Within a moment, Brandon's feet were dangling in the air as Officer Reed carried him back into the house and dropped him onto the couch. And as quickly as Brandon could blink, the officer had tied his hands and feet together with a plastic rope that zipped tight.

"Don't move," Officer Reed commanded as he got up and

walked into the kitchen.

Brandon could hear Officer Reed dialing Grandpa Alvin's phone. He was no doubt calling the school to report he had found Brandon.

Brandon had only a moment to free himself, so he moved quickly. Carefully, he reached into his pocket and pulled out his trusty pocketknife. Extending the large blade, he rubbed it against the plastic bindings around his hands. After a few good strokes, they broke. He then cut the restraints on his feet, and he was free. His heart was pounding again, just like when he had sneaked past the school office. Brandon thought for sure Officer Reed would hear his heartbeat from the next room.

As quietly as he could, Brandon tiptoed to the front door. His hand slowly reached out and grabbed the handle. Then he paused, realizing there was no way he could outrun Officer Reed. *What would Grandpa Alvin do?* he thought.

Officer Reed was still in the kitchen on the phone when the sound of the front door slamming open echoed through the house. A look of panic rushed over the officer's face, and he dropped the phone. He ran into the living room to see the cut restraints on the floor and the door wide open. His eye scrunched up tight, and his teeth gritted together with an awful sound. Like a tiger, he leaped forward into a full sprint, bolting out the door and down the street.

After a moment of silence, Brandon peeked out of the closet door. He could never outrun the officer, but outsmarting him was another matter. Casually, he walked over to the phone lying on the counter.

He picked it up and said with joy, "I'm sorry, but Officer Reed can't talk right now. He's busy running after me."

He smiled and hung up the phone. Then, as stealthily as he could, Brandon sneaked out the back door.

Staying in the shadows of the backyards, Brandon ran for two hours until he reached the edge of town. Beyond the last house were green rolling hills. He hid and looked around for a moment. When he felt the coast was clear, he ran to the top of the nearest hill and then lay down on the other side. Brandon looked back at the quiet town behind him to make sure he wasn't being followed. The quiet little neighborhood seemed to not notice him leaving into the wilderness.

Brandon then set off on his journey to the Color Factory. As he walked up and down the hills, he realized he was now farther than he had ever been from his house. He and his friends were kings of the neighborhood, but he had never been outside his hometown. He was excited but also a little scared deep down.

After a few hours of walking, Brandon started to notice colorful flowers sprinkled across the horizon. Soon he was standing in a whole field of color.

The flowers dancing at his feet were more beautiful than any he had ever seen. Their colors were vibrant purple, red, yellow, and blue. He was overwhelmed with a strong urge to reach down and pick as many as he could carry, but he knew better. He was in the middle of the Painted Fields. Having learned so wisely from his grandfather, Brandon knew that if he picked the flowers, he'd be trapped in the goblin prison.

This meant he was getting closer to the remains of the Color Factory. He was excited. As he walked over the next hill, he saw a peculiar sight. The hill was covered with a vast field of rosebushes. They were small at first but grew taller than trees within a short distance. On the small bushes, the blooming, blushing red roses were the delicate size of grapes. But in the distance, he could see giant flowers that must have been larger than a grown man.

Brandon sat down and studied the map. He didn't see anything about a rosebush forest on the map, and he certainly didn't remember hearing anything about it from Grandpa Alvin. As he gazed at the green jungle before him, he noticed something unusual. Illuminated by the sunlight, there was a piece of concrete hidden in the bushes. It suddenly dawned on him why no one remembered the Color Factory—because its remains were now hidden beneath this tangled mess of thorny vines and giant red distractions.

He had found the Color Factory, but still no one would believe him. He needed more proof. He took out his pocketknife and extended the large blade. He got down on his hands and knees and began crawling through the rosebushes, using the knife to cut the branches in his way. It was slow going. Every so often, he would prick his fingers on the painful thorns of the rosebushes. But in a little while, he had made his way to some crumbling blocks.

The rosebushes were now as thick as trees and were growing right out of the concrete rubble. It was easier to maneuver, as most of the thorny branches were above him. He sifted through the crumbling mess of garbage, looking for any definitive proof. He hoped to find a sign or something that clearly stated it was the Color Factory. So far, all he found were broken building pieces that could have come from anywhere.

As he stepped forward, the ground suddenly gave way, and he fell. Dust clouds filled the air and swirled in the shafts of light breaking into the darkness. Brandon found himself lying in a hallway with pipes running along the walls. He was inside the Color Factory. Not all of it had been destroyed.

Brandon got up and brushed off the dust. He looked at the ceiling. It was littered with little holes shining light down into the hallway. Brandon slowly walked down the hallway, looking for something he could take back to his school as proof. He came upon two doors. The first one opened into a room where the ceiling had collapsed entirely. The second room looked intact, and he carefully walked in and peered around it.

In the back of the dark, dusty room was a grand bed with four posts and green curtains hanging down. Brandon walked over to the bed and slowly opened the curtains. Lying in bed under the covers was a skeleton.

Brandon quickly jumped back in fear. He froze, staring at the dead man as if it would jump up and attack him. After a few deep breaths, Brandon realized the dead man could do him no harm. He slowly inched forward for a closer look.

The skeleton was wearing a brightly colored camouflage military suit with a chest plate of medals. Brandon thought for a moment and then realized this was General Droww. He had never made it out of the Color Factory before it collapsed.

Brandon pulled back the covers and found a book held tightly in the dead man's hands. He reached forward and gently pulled it away.

Wiping the thick dust from the cover, Brandon saw the title of the book was *The Great Sugar War*. He opened the book and saw pen scribbles on the inside cover. It read:

> *Today, a small boy named Alvin discovered a way into the Color Factory to battle the serpents. It took me a while to realize it, but he is the grandson of the boy from the sea. Now I know the Color Factory's reign of terror will soon be over. I am sorry for my part in this horror. I only hope that with my passing, peace and fairness will finally rule through the kingdom.*

> *—General Droww*

Brandon's eyes opened wide. This surely was the proof he needed. He had found the body of General Droww and had a signed confession about the Color Factory and his grandfather's involvement in its destruction. But what did this have to do with Great-Great-Grandfather Otto? Brandon knew his name but knew nothing about him.

Brandon sat in a patch of light peering down at him from a hole in the ceiling. He turned the page to the first chapter, entitled "The Boy from the Sea."

chapter 3

The Boy from the Sea

The choppy blue water broke fast against the side of the ship as it raced through the rough waves. Colonel Droww was at the helm, locked in a fierce battle with a clipper from the Kingdom of Shapes. He was a young, lean man wearing the typical military camouflage of red, orange, yellow, and blue decorated with a small patch of medals on his chest. An ornate green hat with a large purple feather sat proudly atop his head.

The two ships sailed side by side as if in a competition for the finish line. The rumbling booms of the cannons echoed through the air as each vessel fired upon the other.

Behind them was another frigate in the Royal Navy of the Kingdom of Color. It was a slower ship with more firepower. It was struggling to keep up with the other two. In its command was Colonel Grivelt. He was a bear with shaggy brown fur, giant paws with thick claws, and a deep jaw with sharp fangs. He stood a head taller than any man and wore a wide-brimmed hat atop his head, which made him seem even larger. Grivelt stood at the deck edge shouting orders at his crew. Because of his bad knee, he always carried a large knotty walking stick. He sometimes shook it at his subordinates to scare them into submission.

Boom!

The dull gray ship from the south fired again at Droww. It seemed like slow motion as the triangle-shaped object flew straight toward him. All he could do was watch as it hurled closer and closer—and then flew just over his head with a whirling sound. Colonel Droww reached up. His hat was gone. They had blown his hat right off, revealing his short black hair.

He took a quick sigh of relief and then shouted at his crew, "That was too close! Aim hard, and take down their sails!"

"Yes, sir, son of Will the Great!" the men shouted back.

Droww hated when people called him that, but he was not about to make a fuss in the middle of a battle. He watched the main deck of his bright-yellow ship bustle with activity and more shouting.

In a moment, the colorful ship returned fired. Three balls of color launched forward toward the colorless ship bouncing on top of the waves. The first ball was green. It smashed into the side of the ship, exploding planks of gray wood into the air. It left a hole splattered green. The second ball was blue, and it flew through the air, missing the ship entirely. The third ball was pink. It whisked through the main sails like a bullet through paper, leaving a small pink blotch in the gray fabric.

Now it was the enemy's turn. Droww held tightly to the wheel and hoped the next volley would miss entirely. *Boom! Boom! Boom!*

A series of explosions fired a collection of shapes toward the colorful vessel. A swirling star hit dead center in the stern of the ship, creating a massive explosion. Droww blinked from the force and felt his body get tossed into the air. Before he could breathe, a smack of wetness pounded against him as he plunged into the icy depths. Bubbles engulfed him, and Droww flapped his way to the surface.

Colonel Droww perched his head out of the water and spit the salty liquid from his mouth. He was just in time to see his ship succumb to its damage and quickly sink into the blue. Before Droww could even process the great loss, a rush of water pushed him to the side. It was Colonel Grivelt's frigate engaging the enemy. Droww looked up at the vibrant purple ship, an arm's length away. In a moment, the ship had passed completely. Droww struggled to tread water with his heavy clothes and hoped Grivelt's ship would return soon to retrieve him.

Suddenly, Droww caught Grivelt's eyes as he looked back at him bobbing up and down in the waves. Grivelt gave an evil grin and waved his walking stick at Droww as if to say good-bye. In that moment, Colonel Droww knew he was being abandoned.

He and Grivelt had always been competitors. All through military academy, they fought for the top two positions in their class. Sometimes Droww would win out, and sometimes it was Grivelt who won. They even raced across the campus to enlist for the war when the news broke. Now they had a gentlemen's wager on who would become a general first. As Droww watched the two ships disappear over the horizon, he knew that Grivelt had taken his opportunity to eliminate the competition.

Colonel Droww's heart sank as he realized his doom. As he waited for the sharks to find him, he noticed something in the distance in the opposite direction. It was a bright, colorful sail. No one could hear him from so far away, but he shouted for help anyway. His heart grew with hope as the sail drew closer and closer.

In a short while, the boat was upon him. It was a small orange sailboat, barely longer than the height of a man. Its sail was a colorful rainbow that briskly held the wind. Droww was thrilled that not only would he be saved from a watery death but that his rescuer was from the Kingdom of Color. It was far better luck than someone from the Kingdom of Shapes finding him.

When Droww was finally pulled aboard, he was surprised to see its only occupant was a small boy no more than twelve years old.

"Thank you so much for rescuing me," Droww said.

"Anytime," the boy replied. "I'm just glad that I happened upon you. What are you doing out here floating in the middle of the sea?"

"My ship sank," Droww replied as he hung his head low. "It was destroyed by a battleship of shapes, and I'm the only survivor. My name is Colonel Droww, and I'm the son of Will the Great."

The boy looked back at Colonel Droww with curious eyes. "Will the who?"

"You know," the colonel explained. "Will the Great—the

glorious warrior of the Kingdom of Color, the hero of the Color Wars."

"Hmm. Never heard of him. Well, it's a pleasure to meet you, Colonel Droww," the boy stated as he extended his hand to shake. "My name is Otto."

While Colonel Droww extended his hand to shake, he studied Otto from head to toe. He was wearing a blue shirt with a collar and red shorts. He had too much color for anyone from the Kingdom of Shapes.

"It's a pleasure to meet you too, Otto," he said. "You're from the Kingdom of Color, aren't you?"

"The kingdom of where?" Otto answered.

"Of Color," Droww stated. "You're not from the Kingdom of Shapes, are you?"

Otto smiled. "Kingdom of Shapes? Is that a real place?"

Droww looked back at him, perplexed. "It most certainly is," he declared. "We've been at war with them for the last four years."

"I'm sorry," Otto explained. "I come from a land beyond the sea. This boat was a present for my twelfth birthday. When I took it out for the first time, I got caught up in a huge storm. I tossed and turned and lost my bearings. When the storm ended, I couldn't find my way home. I've been sailing for days looking for land. I'm just lucky I was prepared with a few days' worth of food and water, even though I was only planning on sailing for few hours."

Droww smiled at Otto. "Well, I guess it's my turn to save you. I know these waters and can show you the way back to the beautiful green land of the Kingdom of Color."

As Otto and Droww raised the sails and began gliding across the bouncy waves, Otto asked, "So why are you at war with the Kingdom of Shapes?"

"Because they murdered Queen Lusita of the Kingdom of Color," Droww answered.

"Wow!" Otto exclaimed. "I guess that's about as good a reason for war as they come. Why did they do that?"

"There has always been tension and disagreements between the two kingdoms," the colonel explained. "The people of the Kingdom of Color love all the colors in the rainbow. Color is our heart and soul. It is what gives us health and happiness. The people of the Kingdom of Shapes care nothing for color. Instead, they love shapes. They build enormous, complicated, drab buildings. They dress with shapely, colorless trinkets adorning them. So naturally, we've never been able to see eye to eye on many things."

Otto listened intently as they sailed on. A feeling of relief came over him as he spotted land ahead.

"Between our two kingdoms lay the Grasshopper Fields," Colonel Droww continued. "It's a rich, fertile land populated by the simple grasshoppers. Both the Kingdom of Color and the Kingdom of Shapes want to colonize that land and teach the grasshoppers of our better ways. We have divided up the land into different regions, but there have been disagreements over the borders for years."

"So how did they kill the queen?" Otto interrupted.

"The queen? Well, King Fabian had given Queen Lucy, as everyone called her, a brand-new yacht for her birthday. It was the largest, most colorful ship in the fleet—bright pink with red, purple, and blue dots. It was only a pleasure boat and had no weapons of any kind. On her maiden voyage, assassins from the Kingdom of Shapes sneaked aboard the ship and set it ablaze. It burned up and sank into the harbor, killing everyone on board, including Queen Lucy. Thankfully, the king was not on the ship."

"That's awful," stated Otto. "I am so sorry to hear. Maybe there's something I can do to help."

Colonel Droww smiled at Otto. "You already did. You saved my life, and now I'm going to win this war."

chapter 4

War Inspectors

When Otto and Droww reached the shores of the Kingdom of Color, they immediately went to the nearest military base to report that his ship had sunk. As he walked across the base, everyone looked at Colonel Droww in amazement, as if he had come back from the dead. Word had obviously spread of his assumed death. The chattering whispers and wide eyes seemed to give Droww a newfound respect.

When Droww reached the high command office, he turned to Otto. "Wait here. I'll be right out."

As Droww took a step inside the office, he bumped into Colonel Grivelt on his way out. Grivelt's jaw dropped as he saw Droww before him. The two stared at each other silently for a moment, then Droww interjected, "Excuse me, Colonel. I have a war to win."

Droww pushed his way past Grivelt into the office. The shocked bear stood there motionless for a few more seconds, then a nasty scowl came across his face. He continued on his way past Otto. Suddenly, he stopped in his tracks and turned around to look at the young boy. He got down on all fours and approached Otto. He pressed his wet nose against Otto's face and exhaled a deep, stinky breath at him.

"You don't smell like a soldier," the bear growled.

"I'm not a soldier," Otto replied confidently. "I'm Otto. I'm from a land beyond the sea, and I saved Colonel Droww from certain death."

"I see," said Colonel Grivelt. "Then I guess I need to think of a way to thank you." The bear lingered for an awkward moment longer, then stood up and left.

It was the closest Otto had ever been to a bear and certainly the first time he had ever talked to one. He looked around at this strange land and wondered how far he had sailed from his home. The various makeshift tents across the military base were bright magenta, yellow, teal, and maroon. He couldn't figure out where the troops would be fighting that their red, orange, yellow, and blue camouflage would help them at all.

After a few minutes of watching the hustle and bustle on the base, Droww came out of the office. "Come on, Otto," he commanded. "We've got work to do."

"Yes, sir, Colonel Droww," Otto replied with a smile.

Droww smiled back, happy to finally have someone not add "son of Will the Great" to the end of his name.

"We've been charged with escorting the war inspectors to the Grasshopper Fields," the colonel explained.

"What are war inspectors?" the boy inquired.

Droww looked curiously at Otto, amazed by all the things he didn't know. "The war inspectors are the officiates of the war. They are in charge of making sure that everyone involved in the war fights fairly."

Otto looked strangely at Droww. "Fights fairly?" he questioned. "Isn't war what happens when people stop being fair and kill each other?"

"No, no, no, my boy," the colonel replied. "Everything has rules, and we must follow the rules to make sure everyone has an equal chance of everything. You see, we can't have too many troops in one region, because that wouldn't be fair to the other side. And we can't have too few troops, or we wouldn't be allowed to hold that territory."

"Seems rather silly to me," Otto said, giggling.

"Not silly. Civilized," Droww corrected.

The two reached the other side of the base, where there was a horse and carriage. Standing next to it was a small man, shorter than Otto. He had a thick pair of glasses resting atop his large nose. In his hands, he held a clipboard with a stack of paperwork. Otto assumed he was a war inspector.

Colonel Droww leaned over to shake the man's hand. "It's an honor to be assisting you today."

The man looked up from his clipboard and sternly pointed his pen at the colonel. "Don't you think you can sneak anything past me, Colonel," he declared. "I am watching you."

"I wouldn't dream of it, sir," Droww replied as he motioned for everyone to get into the carriage.

The three climbed aboard and were off down the road. Otto

watched as a group of soldiers scurried into a truck and sped away ahead of them.

As they rode slowly down the road, Otto gazed at the landscape. On either side of the road stretched brownish-gray fields. It was certainly not the vibrant, colorful land he was expecting from the colonel's descriptions.

"Colonel Droww, are we in the Kingdom of Color now?" he asked.

"Why, yes, we are, Otto," Droww replied.

"Then why is the land so brown and gray? I was expecting powerful greens, reds, yellow, and blues."

"The ravages of war, I'm afraid," Droww answered. "Ever since the war started, the rains have stopped. With no water, the plants can't grow. With no plants growing, there is no color."

Otto looked up at the sky. There was a thick cloud cover for as far as he could see in every direction. "Well, there are plenty of clouds. Maybe it will rain soon," he stated.

"I'm afraid not, Otto," Droww interjected. "Those clouds have been there since the war started. Military intelligence thinks the Kingdom of Shapes has extracted the water from the clouds to keep it from raining. That way, we'll run low of color and won't be able to continue fighting in the war."

Otto studied the sky, wondering how anyone could keep the clouds from raining. From his lessons in school, he knew that clouds were made of water. So if someone took the water away, there would be no clouds at all. Otto thought how strange the Kingdom of Color was and wondered what other weird things he'd encounter next.

Just then, they rolled into the first camp. It was a small military base with only a few tents of turquoise, lime green, and crimson. Standing in front of the road were ten soldiers neatly lined up, and the truck from earlier was parked behind a tent. The carriage stopped, and they all got out.

The little round man looked at his clipboard, then back at Colonel Droww. "Every camp must have exactly fifty men to meet the guidelines," he stated. "Or else you will need to forfeit this region."

Otto looked at the ten men lined up. It wasn't even close to fifty soldiers. He wondered how Droww would react when the war inspector would shut down the camp for not following the rules.

Otto watched as the tiny man wobbled up to the first man in the line. He pointed at him with his pen and said, "One." He continued moving down the line, counting as he went. "Two, three, four, five."

When the inspector was on five, the first three men in line stepped back and scurried behind the line to the other side.

After the inspector counted the tenth and last man, he continued down the line and pointed to the first man he had started with. "Eleven," he counted.

Otto's jaw dropped. He was stunned as he saw the war inspector continue down the line, counting higher and higher. As he passed the men, they each got out of line, sneaked around the back, and got back in line at the other end. The rule maker with the thick glasses never seemed to notice. After a few minutes, the inspector had reached fifty and scribbled away on his clipboard.

"Excuse me, sir," Otto interrupted. "Did you say the base needs fifty men?"

The inspector squinted and glared at Otto as if seeing him for the first time. "And who are you?" he snarked.

"Um, I'm Otto, sir," he replied. "I'm—"

Colonel Droww stepped in and said, "He's my assistant."

The little man looked up at Droww. "Oh, okay. Well, yes. Every base needs exactly fifty men."

Otto glanced at the ten men lined up on the road. "And you don't see any problems with this camp?" he questioned.

"I do," the war inspector replied. "You are not wearing a uniform. Every soldier must be properly dressed to protect his knees from dirt."

Otto did a double take at the soldiers. They all looked nervous and stared at Otto as if to shout with their eyes, "Shut up!"

Otto continued, "So how many men did you count?"

The inspector studied his clipboard for a moment, then stated, "Fifty men exactly. This base is up to snuff." He then pointed at Otto intently and declared, "But you are not up to snuff. You've got five minutes to be dressed in appropriate wear, or I'll shut this whole war down."

Otto couldn't believe what he had heard. Years ago, one of his neighbors lost his mind, and some men in white coats came and took him away. He never knew where they took him. Now Otto was beginning to think they took him and all the other crazy people to the Kingdom of Color.

Before Otto could utter a word, the soldiers grabbed him and whisked him away into a tent. And before the war inspector could blink, they had Otto back by the carriage, dressed in the same colorful camouflage.

The war inspector glanced from his clipboard and gazed at Otto strangely. "Who are you?" he questioned.

"Um, I'm Otto, sir," he replied. "Colonel Droww's assistant."

"Oh," the little man stated. "You look much better than his other assistant."

"So is everything in order, sir?" Otto asked.

The inspector spent a long while studying his clipboard. "Everything is good here. Next base," he announced.

With that, Colonel Droww, the war inspector, and Otto climbed in the carriage and were off. As they rode, Otto looked back and saw the ten nervous soldiers scramble into the truck hidden behind the tent. They then raced down the road past the horse and carriage. When they reached the next base, Otto was not the least bit surprised to see the same ten men lined up in a row. Otto kept his mouth shut and watched this same process unfold at every base they visited. The same ten men drove from camp to camp ahead of them. The same ten men moved from one end of the line to the other as the war inspector counted. And sure enough, he counted exactly fifty men at every base. When the day was over, the war inspector had approved each base. He gave the Kingdom of Color the green light for war.

27

chapter 5

An Empty Pyramid

"Are you ready for war, my boy?" Colonel Droww asked Otto.

Otto watched as the war inspector rode over the horizon and out of sight. He then looked down at himself in his new army fatigues. He looked surprisingly good in the colorful disguise. He checked his pocket to verify he still had his trusty knife with him.

"I guess I'm ready, Colonel Droww," he replied.

"Good thing, my boy," the colonel said as he patted him on the head.

"But there is one thing I don't quite understand, Colonel," Otto said. "How do you expect to win a war with only ten soldiers and me?"

Droww chuckled and explained, "We've got more than ten soldiers. In these regions, we only need a few soldiers to maintain our hold. Our important soldiers are fighting on other fronts."

"But Colonel, we visited thirteen bases with the inspector, and they needed fifty men each. So there should have been . . . ah . . . six hundred and fifty soldiers. We only had the same ten."

Colonel Droww smiled at the naive boy. He got down on one knee, placed his hand on Otto's shoulder, and explained, "Truth is always the first casualty of war."

Otto nodded that he understood, even though he didn't. As he, Droww, and the ten soldiers all piled into the truck and drove away to somewhere, Otto's mind was fixed upon Droww's words. All the heroes Otto had grown up admiring were virtuous. They proudly stated they would never lie, even if telling the truth resulted in their punishment. And now lost in this world of magnificent color—which was, in reality, rather muted and dull—Otto was so confused. It left a bad taste in his mouth. For the first time, he truly longed for home.

Otto didn't pay attention to where they were going until they came to a screeching halt. When he looked up, Otto saw the most amazing thing. Standing a short distance away was an enormous pyramid. It was taller than any building he had ever seen. It was made of bricks that each must have been the size of a small house. The bricks were all dull gray, but it looked as though people had painted the first several layers in flamboyant purples, yellows, and oranges.

The pyramid was sitting in the middle of a city—or at least Otto thought it was a city. There were hundreds of grasshoppers walking around that were as big as his parents. The sea of bugs stretched as far as he could see in every direction. It took Otto a few moments to realize there were no other buildings anywhere around.

"Where are we?" Otto inquired.

"Deep in enemy territory," Droww explained as they got out of the truck. "We are here on a goodwill mission to show the grasshoppers just how much better color is than shapes. "

Otto watched as the soldiers came out of the back of the truck with big colorful crates of pink, cyan, and maroon. Before he knew it, an endless line of grasshoppers came up to the painted boxes. Each grasshopper received a vibrant bag from the soldiers. The bags were filled with candy and goodies. Droww walked up and down the line, spouting the wonderful benefits of color to the eager listeners.

A little overwhelmed at the sight, Otto took a seat on a rock and watched the grasshoppers wander by after receiving their bags of goodies. They were tall, lean, and all they carried were the bags from Droww and the soldiers.

Otto watched as they ate some candy from the bags, then tossed the wrappers onto the ground and walked off. The ground was now littered with colorful garbage sprinkled across the fields of matted-down brown grass.

When one grasshopper dropped a wrapper right at Otto's feet, Otto picked it up. He held it toward the offender. "Hey there! Do you think you could put this in the trash?"

The grasshopper stopped and looked at Otto strangely. He wasn't sure if the grasshopper had even understood him.

After an awkward moment of looking at each other, the grasshopper meekly inched up to Otto and took the wrapper back. He looked Otto up and down carefully and muttered, "Thank you, sir." Then he turned and walked away.

Otto continued to watch the grasshopper as he scampered away. No more than ten steps away, the grasshopper dropped the wrapper back onto the ground and continued on his way.

Otto shook his head in amazement.

"First time seeing a grasshopper?" a raspy voice asked. Otto turned around and saw an old woman standing behind him. She was wearing brown clothes with several colorful patches. A purple bandanna was wrapped tightly around her head, covering the long white scraggly hair flowing down the sides of her tanned, wrinkled face. On her back, she wore a large overflowing backpack that seemed to weigh more than she did.

"Yes. I mean, no . . . I mean . . ." he stumbled. "Well, we've got many grasshoppers back home, but none as big as a man, and none that talk. Are all the grasshoppers in the Kingdom of Color this big?"

"You're far from the Kingdom of Color, my dear," the old woman corrected. "You're deep within the Grasshopper Fields." She pointed to the gigantic pyramid and explained, "You see that pyramid? It was built by the Kingdom of Shapes as a gift to the grasshoppers. This is in the heart of Shape Territory. Didn't they teach you anything in color school?"

"Color school?" Otto stuttered. "I didn't go to color school. My name is Otto, and I come from a land beyond the sea."

The old woman smiled. "You don't say. I haven't met anyone from beyond the sea before." She then took her bag off her back, pulled out some support poles, and quickly configured the fabric into a chair. She sat down next to Otto. He was amazed to see a backpack transform into a chair in mere seconds.

"My name is Nellie Trailbender, but everyone just calls me Aunt Nellie."

"It's a pleasure to meet you, Aunt Nellie," Otto replied politely.

Aunt Nellie reached into her bag and pulled out a long wooden spoon. Using the handle end, she drew a circle into the ground.

"This is the Kingdom of Color," she explained. "The northern part is the Red Berry Forest, where all the fruits of the kingdom are grown. The southern part is Vegetable Valley, where all the

vegetables are grown. On the eastern border are the Shadow Mountains. Beyond there, nothing grows. On the northern and western borders are the vast waters of the sea. And on the southern border are the Grasshopper Fields, so called because the only ones who live here are thousands of grasshoppers—and me, of course. I was here long before the grasshoppers."

Otto smiled at the old woman. He wondered how old she might be but knew better than to ever ask a woman her age.

"South of the Grasshopper Fields is the Kingdom of Shapes," she stated as she continued to draw.

"So what do the grasshoppers think of the war between the two kingdoms on their land?" Otto interrupted.

A sly smile perked across the old woman's face. "You are a smart boy," she said. "Now I know why Droww is keeping you around."

Otto smiled at the compliment.

"If you ask the grasshoppers in the northern part of the fields, they would probably say they support the Kingdom of Color," she continued. "And the southern grasshoppers would probably say the Kingdom of Shapes. But in reality, they care little for either side. They just like receiving free stuff."

Otto thought for a moment, then asked, "So which side do you fight for?"

Aunt Nellie reached out and pinched his chin. "Oh, I don't fight, honey," she stated. "I stay out of their little war. I try to teach the grasshoppers of a third and better way."

"A third side?" he questioned.

"Not a side," she corrected. "A *way*. I encourage the grasshoppers to live in harmony with both colors and shapes. You see, the grasshoppers are a simple bunch. They have no clothes, have no houses, and have no beds. They simply walk from place to place within the Grasshopper Fields. When they're hungry, they reach down and eat something. When they're tired, they lie down wherever they are and sleep. They never think to the future, only of the moment."

Aunt Nellie motioned to the pyramid. "King Rhombus of the Kingdom of Shapes thought a powerful, shapely building would convince them of the importance of his way. Then the Army of Color came and painted it as high as they could reach to convince the grasshoppers of their way of life. And now the building sits empty. The grasshoppers do not understand the need for it when they have everything they want

at their fingertips in the bountiful fields."

Otto looked up at the colossal building and blurted out, "You mean that pyramid is completely empty inside?"

"Yep," Nellie answered. "So I try to teach them of the balance between shapes and color. I also try to teach them to plan ahead for their future, for when the fields aren't so abundant. They need to plant crops and store food, and they need to find or build shelters to protect themselves when the weather is dangerous."

Otto thought for a moment, then replied, "So who is winning the war for the minds of the grasshoppers? The Kingdom of Color, the Kingdom of Shapes, or Aunt Nellie?"

"The grasshoppers are winning, I'm afraid." She laughed. "They are a stubborn bunch. In the end, no one will be able to convince them of anything other than what they know."

chapter 6

Sugar Bubbles

As Otto and Aunt Nellie talked, a small tremor caught their attention. They both looked down at the map Nellie had drawn and saw the dirt vibrating. Within a moment, the patch of ground was shaking so hard that the picture disappeared completely in the crumbles.

Suddenly, a small glistening white bubble popped out of the dirt. It was about the size of a pumpkin. It seemed to move ever so slightly as if it were breathing. The surface was a sparkling dance of white glitter that swirled in circular motion. It seemed wet, as if it were a liquid, but it clearly had a three-dimensional shape.

Otto looked at Aunt Nellie in amazement and confusion. "And what is this?" he asked.

"I don't know, my boy," she replied. "In all my many years, I have never seen such a thing."

This land kept getting stranger and stranger. First he landed in the so-called Kingdom of Color that seemed to be mostly brown and gray. Then he met the gigantic grasshoppers that talked like people. And now there was this mysterious shiny ball that sprang from the ground like a flower. He thought it might be just another strange thing in this strange land, but something just didn't feel right in his stomach. That was when it hit him. This bubble had a definite shape but no color. Maybe it was a trap or some kind of a weapon of the Kingdom of Shapes.

As soon as this thought ran through his head, Otto heard a commotion shoot like lightning through the crowd of grasshoppers. Otto and Nellie looked up to see more bubbles. Hundreds of bubbles were sprinkled across the golden fields. The sounds of terrified arguing bubbled up in the mass of grasshoppers. The neatly formed line of grasshoppers waiting for the colorful bags burst into a scattered mess, leaving the soldiers alone in the confusion.

Otto jumped up and ran over to Colonel Droww. "I don't think this is good, Colonel!" he shouted. "I think it's a weapon of the Kingdom of Shapes."

Panic rushed over the soldiers' faces. To reassure them, Colonel Droww piped in, "I doubt that, my boy. The Kingdom of Shapes doesn't have any weapons like this. This must be a natural phenomenon."

"Really?" Otto retorted, unconvinced.

"Really, Otto," Droww said confidently.

"Then what are these bubbles, and where do they come from?" Otto demanded.

"Hmm," the colonel said. "Let's go find out."

Droww walked over to the nearest bubble. His troops followed close behind. He knelt down next to the bubble for a closer look. Otto sat down beside him to see for himself. Filled with anxiety, the soldiers stayed a good distance away just in case it exploded. Suddenly, a crowd of grasshoppers formed around them. One brave grasshopper crept up and knelt down on the other side of the bubble from Colonel Droww. As he studied the sparkling ball, Droww rubbed his hand across his face. The grasshopper followed suit and rubbed his hands across his face. The colonel took a deep breath, then leaned in close. The grasshopper did the same, as if he were Droww's reflection in a mirror. With each action from Droww, the grasshopper repeated it. Otto got distracted by the comical display and almost forgot about the bubble.

Colonel Droww reached into his belt and pulled out a knife. He started to scrape it gently across the bubble's surface. The grasshopper picked up a stick from the ground and did the same. The exterior of the bubble felt soft and wet. Droww continued by carefully poking the bubble with his knife. It firmly held its shape as the knife gently dived inside. The grasshopper's misshapen stick entered the bubble just as smoothly as the sharp knife.

Slowly, Droww moved the knife back and forth through the bubble. He felt little resistance, as if he were stirring a thick soup. He then sliced through the glistening bubble faster and faster. Nothing changed except that swirling circles formed on the surface of the bubble like storm clouds in the sky.

Droww removed the knife. He sat up and thought for a moment. The crowd of grasshoppers leaned in, eager to learn the mystery of the bubbles. Colonel Droww then took his finger and poked it into the white ball.

"Colonel!" Otto exclaimed. "What are you doing?"

Colonel Droww pulled out his finger. It was lightly covered with the gooey substance. Otto's eyes went wide when Droww lifted his finger to his nose and sniffed. And before Otto could say anything, Droww shoved his finger into his mouth.

"Sir!" Otto cried out.

"I knew it," Colonel Droww announced. "Sugar! These are sugar bubbles!"

As Droww swallowed the sweet goodness of the bubble, a burst of blue raced across his face. Otto glanced at the grasshopper, who had also poked his finger into the bubble. As he pulled his finger from his mouth, a rush of pink glowed on his face.

An explosion of thunder rolled across the crowds as the grasshoppers cheered. Before Otto knew what was happening, all the grasshoppers scampered around the sugar bubbles and began consuming as much as they could. Some scooped out handfuls at a time and shoved them into their faces. Others leaned right over and licked the sparkling bubbles. Otto even saw one grasshopper use a straw to drink from a bubble like a milkshake. As he gazed upon the fields across the horizon, Otto saw that all the grasshoppers were kneeling down and gorging themselves with sweet pleasure.

Otto turned around and saw the once-scared soldiers huddled around their own bubbles, eating as much sugar as they could. As they ate the sugar, their faces danced with color.

"Come on, Otto!" Colonel Droww exclaimed. "You must try some."

"I don't know, Colonel Droww," Otto replied. "I'm still

worried about it."

The colonel held out a handful to Otto. "Just one taste, boy. That is an order."

Otto was torn. He loved sugar as much as the next boy, but he still felt it was some kind of trap. But the temptation was too great. Otto followed his orders and took a taste. It was simply delicious. A magical swirl of sweetness danced in his mouth. It was like nothing he had tasted before. He wanted more. Otto got down on his knees and began eating at the same bubble as Colonel Droww.

Within a few minutes, all the fear had left Otto. There was no way such tasty sugar could be dangerous. He took a handful and offered it up to Aunt Nellie. "You have to try some. It's simply marvelous," he said.

Aunt Nellie looked at him with a suspicious eye. "No thank you, my dear," she replied. "I'm not one for sweets."

Otto shrugged and went back to his feast. The sound of eating echoed through the fields as everyone filled their bellies with happiness.

As night fell, a spectacular party spread across the fields. The sky was still covered with thick clouds, but the spheres of sugar sparkled like disco balls. It was like partying among the stars. Music played loudly as the grasshoppers danced around the balls of delight. And all through the night, bursts of magnificent color sparkled across everyone's face as they gorged themselves with handfuls of sugar.

This was much different from any party Otto had been to before. All his parties were held during the day and consisted of games such as Red Rover or Pin the Tail. Otto had never stayed up so late before. It was exhilarating to experience wild dancing to fast-paced music. The lights were swirling, and the sugar bubbles were vibrating to the beat of the drums. This was a grown-up party, and Otto liked it. He decided then and there that he wanted all his parties from now on to be like this one.

chapter 7

The Sleeping City

Otto awoke the next morning with a pounding headache. The bright light of the sun beat down on him as if it were yelling at him to get up. After trying to block out the sun with his arm, Otto finally, slowly, rose to meet the hammering day. As soon as he pushed himself to a sitting position, a throbbing pain rushed into his head. He felt the whole world spin. He had to lay back down before he lost his lunch. His entire body tingled from the effects of that sweet, sticky substance.

It took a couple of minutes for the feeling of deep sickness to subside. Otto looked around and realized he had no idea where he was. He was not at any of the army bases or near the empty pyramid. He was sitting in the middle of a field surrounded by sleeping grasshoppers intermingled with sparkling sugar bubbles. He thought hard and couldn't remember how he had gotten there. Looking around, he didn't recognize anything.

Otto tried to retrace his steps of the night before. But for the life of him, he couldn't remember anything. The entire night was a complete blur. His last solid memory was looking at Aunt Nellie as she declined the sugar. After that, he could recall only vague images that seemed to be from a movie he had seen long,

long ago. There had been dancing. Then the sensation of falling echoed in his head. Had he jumped off something? Had he been thrown?

As he rubbed his face, trying to remember the events of the night, he realized his cheek was sore. He looked down at the ground and saw several hand-sized balls of sugar sprinkled across the matted grass. Images of a sugar ball fight popped into his head. He couldn't remember how it started or even if he had won or lost. But with the feeling on the side of his face, he knew he had been involved.

The glistening sugar bubbles were still sparkling with light across the field. They seemed to magnify the bright light of the sun, creating a strange glow across the ground. The sweet, sticky twinkle made Otto feel sick to his stomach. All he could think of was drinking a large glass of cold water to wash the taste from his mouth.

The fields were littered with sleeping grasshoppers like confetti after a parade. Otto walked to a nearby grasshopper to ask if he knew where they were. As he approached, he noticed the giant bug was coated in shiny glitter across his face and body, almost as if he had taken a bath in sugar. Otto shook the grasshopper to wake him.

"Hey there!" he shouted. "Wake up! Do you know where we are? Do you have any water?"

The grasshopper snorted loudly and followed it with a

rumbling snore, without waking up at all. Otto stumbled a few steps over to the next grasshopper, but he wouldn't move either.

Just then, Otto noticed one of the grasshoppers at the top of the next hill sitting up and holding his head. He jumped up to head over to him, but a pounding sensation and the taste of vomit rushed over him. Otto fell to his knees and watered the ground with a disgusting hot, sparkling brown liquid. After wiping the gunk from the side of his mouth, Otto crawled up the hill to the stirring grasshopper.

"Good morning," Otto said as he stumbled.

"Ugh. Go away," the grasshopper replied. "My head hurts."

"You too?" Otto said.

"Ah! Not so loud," he answered, wincing at the sound of Otto's voice.

"Sorry," Otto whispered. "Do you have any water?"

The grasshopper looked down at his hands, then at the ground around him. He had nothing. "Nope," he replied.

"Do you know where the pyramid is?" Otto inquired.

The sluggish bug rubbed his head some more, then pointed to the east. "The shape is over there," he answered.

Otto pushed himself to his feet and began walking east. As he stumbled through the tall grasses, he looked down at the sleeping grasshoppers that lay throughout the field. Each one was sound asleep and covered with the same white glitter. It was almost as if someone had painted them all with the sugar from the bubbles.

After a few minutes, Otto came across another grasshopper who was awake and stumbling around. That grasshopper didn't have any water either. Now Otto was getting very thirsty.

Beyond the next hill, he saw an enormous building. He was glad to see he was getting close to the pyramid. But when he stopped to focus his eyes, he realized it wasn't the pyramid. It was something different. It was a giant sugar bubble. Most of the bubbles popping out of the ground were no bigger than beach balls, but this one was huge. It was larger than his house back home.

It was perfectly round and protruding out of the ground just like the others. The sphere also had the same glistening white sparkle as the others.

Otto stopped at another grasshopper sitting up among the sleeping masses. "What is that?" he asked.

The groggy grasshopper looked up from his hands and replied, "It's a sugar bubble. Where have you been?"

"I know that," Otto replied. "But why is it so big?"

"Well, if you knew that, then why did you ask?" the grasshopper muttered. "Stupid boy."

"Why is it so big?" Otto persisted.

The grasshopper looked at the giant bubble again. "'Cause

it's got lots of good sugar," he said.

Otto shook his head and realized this was going nowhere fast. "Okay. Do you at least have any water?" Otto asked hopefully.

"Water?" the grasshopper replied rudely. "What do I look like, the water fairy?"

The grasshopper was covered from head to toe with a light coat of sparkling glitter. "You do kinda look like a fairy," Otto stated.

The grasshopper gave him a scowl, then lay back down on the ground.

Forgetting the grouchy grasshopper, Otto pressed on to the east, looking for the pyramid. As he walked, he kept looking back at the giant sugar bubble. He didn't know what to expect but knew something was not right about it. After it was out of sight, Otto finally saw the pyramid in the distance. He was relieved. He hoped Colonel Droww, the soldiers, and even Aunt Nellie were there. As he walked on, he wondered how he had gotten so far away.

When he reached the top of the next hill, Otto was amazed at the sight. There must have been thousands of grasshoppers sleeping at the foot of the pyramid. They were stacked on top of each other in a giant, snoring mess. A few were awake and wandering through the crowds of slumbering bugs. For a split second, it reminded him of the aftermath of a battlefield in one of his history books.

A smile spread across his face when he saw Aunt Nellie sitting in her chair next to a campfire. Otto rushed through the jungle of sleeping grasshoppers as quickly as he could. His head was still throbbing, and he felt a slimy, icky feeling pulsating through his whole body.

"Good morning, Aunt Nellie," he said when he reached her. "Do you have any water?"

"Sure I do," she replied. She reached into her bag and pulled out a water bottle. She handed it to Otto, and he poured it down his throat as if he had just crossed the desert. As he sat down next to her, Aunt Nellie handed him an apple. "Here, my boy," she said. "You need to eat some good food."

"Thanks," Otto mumbled. He devoured the apple. Getting a bellyful of water and an apple made him feel a thousand times better. The pain in his head started to go away, and he no longer felt the powerful sugar flowing through his veins.

He looked around at the sleeping city of grasshoppers. "Why is everyone sleeping?" he asked.

"Sugar coma," Aunt Nellie said instantly. "This is what happens when all you eat is sugar."

"Really?" Otto asked.

"Yes, my dear," she continued. "Sugar gives you a burst of color and energy, and it makes you feel like the king of the world. But it does that by robbing you of your real energy. Soon you lose your energy and color."

Just then, Otto looked down at himself and realized he looked different. With the gray cloud cover, he hadn't quite noticed it before, but his color had changed. His clothes and skin were now faded and grayish.

"My color! What happened?" he shouted.

"Don't worry, Otto," Aunt Nellie reassured. "Just eat some good fruits and vegetables, and your true color will return."

She handed him a pear from her bag. Otto ate it as fast as he could, hoping to restore his beautiful color.

As Otto and Aunt Nellie talked about the importance of fruits and vegetables, Colonel Droww awoke and stumbled over to them. Droww brewed himself a cup of coffee over the fire while half listening to them.

45

After he got a few hot sips into his body, he interrupted, "Do you remember anything from last night, Otto?"

"Sorry, Colonel Droww," Otto said. "Last night is a blur."

"For me too," Droww replied.

"Last thing I remember," Otto explained, "I was talking with Nellie. Then I woke up in the middle of nowhere in a field of sleeping grasshoppers. It took me an hour to find my way back here."

Otto thought some more, then suddenly remembered the giant sugar bubble.

"Colonel Droww, I found a giant sugar bubble just over that hill," he blurted out. "It's bigger than a house."

Colonel Droww looked at Otto strangely. After listening intently to Otto describing the new discovery, he decided they needed to investigate. He called over one of his soldiers and barked, "Get the troops! We need to investigate this giant sugar bubble."

"Yes, sir, son of Will the Great," the soldier replied as he ran to get the other troops.

Colonel Droww scowled at the soldier. He wanted to order the men to stop calling him that, but he knew it wouldn't do any good.

Otto, Colonel Droww, and the soldiers suited up and marched off toward the peculiar find. Together, they walked over the next hill to see the giant sparkling sugar bubble coming out of the ground. It took a moment for their eyes to adjust to the white light radiating off the enormous sphere. Then they noticed a swarming commotion surrounding the bubble.

A group of sparkling people was scurrying around the bubble. They were shaped like humans, but their features were undefined. They seemed to be made of the same glittery substance as the sugar bubbles. Otto watched as more of the beings walked right out of the giant sugar bubble as if it were a doorway. Then they lined up just as Otto had seen Colonel Droww's soldiers do.

These weren't ordinary people. They were soldiers. They were sugar soldiers.

chapter 8

The Battle of Grasshopper Fields

Before Droww's group could act, the sugar soldiers spotted them. Instantly, the swarm of sparkling soldiers came rushing toward them.

Colonel Droww only had time to yell, "Draw your weapons!"

But before the Army of Color soldiers could react, the sugar soldiers tackled them like a powerful wave.

The soldiers wrestled on the ground in a flurry of fists and kicks. Otto struggled under the weight of the full-grown man made of sugar. Like the bubbles, the sugar soldiers were made of slippery goo. Otto was small, but he was fast. With his opponent so slick, it was easy for Otto to roll to his stomach. Otto then lifted his hips, forcing the weight of the sugar soldier onto his upper body. From there, it was a cinch to slip out the side and reverse positions to the top.

Droww and two of the soldiers had made it to their feet. The colonel quickly drew his sword and swung it wildly at the enemy to create some space between them. When one of the sugar soldiers charged, Colonel Droww took a sharp swing at his right arm, severing it completely. The glistening white arm landed on the ground and crumbled into a pile of raw sugar. Droww smiled at besting his opponent. But before he could swing again, the stubby arm of the sugar soldier wiggled and grew back into a full arm as if nothing had happened.

Colonel Droww froze, shocked by the regenerating enemy. But he was determined to defeat them, so he swung again. His fast blade cut diagonally across the sugar soldier's chest. But once again, the soldier quickly healed himself. Droww jumped up and kicked the dazzling soldier in the face. The soldier was stunned, and Droww attacked again. In a single motion, he slashed off the left arm, then spun around and cut off the right. As the sugar soldier concentrated on growing both his arms, Colonel Droww raised his blade and forcefully swung through the enemy's neck. The sugar soldier fell to his knees, then to the ground in a crumbling mess.

Droww quickly glanced around and saw Otto, who was now on top of his opponent. "Get off him!" Droww yelled at Otto.

Otto quickly jumped off and rolled away as Colonel Droww

swiftly removed the sugar soldier's head. Otto felt excited—Droww had figured out how to defeat them. They were winning the battle. Being on the wrestling team at school, Otto knew the familiar feeling when he knew he was better than his opponent. With the great Colonel Droww on his side, he knew they would win.

Suddenly, a strange sight caught Otto's eye. He noticed three sugar soldiers had pinned one of Droww's soldiers down to the ground. Two sugar soldiers held the man's arms, and the third sat on his chest. The one on his chest leaned down and pressed his face against the soldier's. The soldier from the Kingdom of Color began to convulse. A glowing glitter spread throughout his body. Faster than Otto could blink his eyes, the soldier transformed completely into sugar. He arose as a new sugar soldier.

"Look out!" Otto screamed. "The sugar soldiers can turn you into one of them!"

Colonel Droww heard him and whirled around in time to see two more of his soldiers transform into the enemy. The remaining soldiers were all on their feet. They created a line. They all swung their swords wildly to keep the sugar soldiers from getting too close. Piles of crumbling sugar collected at their feet as they chopped off hands, arms, and feet. Having no weapon, Otto stayed behind them, waiting for the end.

Otto was now more scared than he had been before. The thought of being turned into a sugar monster echoed through his brain. Time seemed to move in slow motion. He could hear every chime of his heart beating in his ear. At least they were winning. They had lost three soldiers, but they were able to strike back against the sugar soldiers, who were down to five.

Otto eyes fixated on the giant sugar bubble. More and more sugar soldiers poured out of the glistening ball and lined up, waiting for orders to strike. There must have been at least twenty.

"Colonel Droww!" Otto yelled. "Look at the bubble! Look at the bubble!"

Droww glanced at the bubble between swings and saw their impending doom. His heart sank, as he knew they could not defeat twenty more.

"Fall back to the pyramid!" he commanded.

The group quickly made its way back down the hill. They sprinted toward the city of sleeping grasshoppers. Otto glanced back, and it seemed the sugar soldiers were not following them. Instead, they had turned their attention to the sleeping grasshoppers on the hill, who had amazingly slept through their battle. One by one, they were turning them into more sugar soldiers.

As Otto, Droww, and the color soldiers ran into the sea of sleeping bugs, they screamed as loudly as they could to wake up the grasshoppers. They even tried to stop and shake a few but had no luck.

"We have to wake them up," Droww commanded. "This will be a slaughter."

Otto saw Aunt Nellie still sitting by the fire. As fast as lightning, he ran over to her. "War is upon us!" he exclaimed. "We need to wake everyone up now!"

"I'm sorry, Otto," she explained. "I'm not taking sides in your little war."

"I know," stated Otto, "but an army of sugar soldiers is just over that hill. If we don't wake these grasshoppers, they'll all be transformed into sugar. Perhaps you too."

Aunt Nellie held her hand over her mouth and gasped.

"Quick—do you have any more water?" Otto pleaded.

"Yes. Always," she replied. She reached in her bag and handed him a water bottle.

Otto took the bottle and splashed some water onto the face of a nearby grasshopper. Unfortunately, it didn't work. The grasshopper continued snoring away as if nothing had happened.

"It's not working!" Otto exclaimed. "But they need to wake up!"

"I have an idea," Aunt Nellie said as she reached into her bag again. In a flash, she pulled out a small golden alarm clock with two bells on top. "Here, try this," she ordered. "Nothing breaks a sleep better than the annoying sound of an alarm clock."

Otto took the clock. He gave it a few good winds in the back, set the time, and waited. After what seemed to be the longest minute of his life, the alarm clock burst into action. It blared its powerful ring through the air. The noise was so loud that it made Otto jump with shock. All the grasshoppers nearby suddenly raised their heads. It worked. It actually worked! Otto jumped for joy.

As quickly as he could, Otto ran through the fields of slumbering giant grasshoppers, ringing the alarm over and over again to wake up more and more of them. Colonel Droww and his soldiers followed behind, warning each grasshopper of the impending battle. After an hour had passed, many of the grasshoppers had awoken and were preparing for battle. Otto and Droww pressed on to wake the rest.

Then without warning, a clatter arose from the edges of the fields. Otto and Droww stopped and looked at the commotion. The sugar soldiers were attacking. They were too late.

The sugar soldiers had amassed an army at least one hundred strong. Otto hoped the sugar soldiers would not be a match for the thousands of grasshoppers now engaging them in battle.

"Otto, continue waking the grasshoppers," Droww ordered. "I need to take my soldiers into battle."

"Yes, sir, Colonel Droww," he replied with a salute.

The colonel smiled at Otto. It felt great to finally know someone who always called him by his name. Deep down, above all else, Colonel Droww liked to keep Otto around for that reason alone.

In a flash, Droww and his men charged into the center of the battle. Otto moved as fast as he could to wake more and more grasshoppers. As he navigated through the sleeping piles of grasshoppers, Otto reassured himself that each grasshopper he woke would strengthen the chance of their victory.

chapter 9

Escape to Vegetable Valley

After two hours, Otto had finally awakened all the grasshoppers sleeping around the pyramid. As he paused to catch his breath, he gazed upon the raging battle. Sugar soldiers were fighting grasshoppers as far as he could see in every direction.

In the sea of fighting creatures, Otto noticed that half were grasshoppers and half were sugar soldiers. A sinking feeling gathered in Otto's stomach. Otto looked closer and saw grasshopper after grasshopper being turned into a sugar soldier. There were now thousands of sugar soldiers. The Army of Color was losing the battle. Soon the sugar army would swallow them all. He needed to find Colonel Droww.

As fast as he could, Otto ran through the battlefield. Grasshoppers were fighting sugar soldiers all around him. He ducked under swinging arms trying to hit him. He jumped over fallen bodies of crumbling sugar. The rumbling noise of battle resonated all around him. He didn't know which way was what. He didn't even know where Colonel Droww was. Maybe he was running toward him, or maybe he was running in the opposite direction. He just kept running, hoping he had luck on his side.

After a few minutes of dodging his way through the fighting,

Otto began to worry. What if Colonel Droww had turned into a sugar soldier? Then he would never find him, and Otto would be lost in this strange land forever.

All at once, everything went black. Otto felt a pain throughout his entire body. He opened his eyes. He was lying on the ground. He had been tackled by a sugar soldier who was now lying on top of him with all his weight. Otto couldn't move beneath the giant sticky man. The soldier leaned in to press his face against Otto's.

Otto struggled desperately to get free. The feet of grasshoppers and sugar soldiers danced all around him. He looked to the left and saw the alarm clock. It must have gone flying in the force of the attack. It was more than an arm's length away. There was no way he could reach it. He glanced to his right and saw the water bottle Aunt Nellie had given him. The top was off, and water had spilled onto the ground. The silver bottle glimmered in the light just beyond his fingertips. He struggled to reach a little farther.

The face of the sugar soldier pressed against his check. He could feel a strange tingle in his head, which began spreading through his body. With the tip of his finger, he carefully rolled the water bottle closer until he could grab it. Then he swung it as hard as he could against the sugar soldier's face. The soldiers' head jerked back from the impact, and water splashed onto his face. The sugar soldier sat up and held his face in pain. Otto watched as the soldier's face melted away until his head was completely gone. The lifeless body swayed to the side and fell to the ground next to Otto in a crumbly mess.

Otto sat up in relief and checked himself over. The chaos of the battle raged all around him, but he was focused on the melting sugar soldier. *Water.* Water was the key.

Now he really had to find Colonel Droww and tell him their weakness. He felt a new surge of energy and jumped to his feet. He continued running through the fighting masses in search of the colonel.

As Otto dodged through the horde, he saw Aunt Nellie out of the corner of his eye. She was lying on the ground with a glistening sugar soldier on top of her. Otto stopped in his tracks and raced to her as fast as he could. But when he threw his body into the enemy to tackle him, he bounced off as if he had run into a wall. The sugar soldier didn't seem to notice Otto. He was only focused on Nellie.

Otto thought fast. He needed water. He looked down and saw Aunt Nellie's bag lying on the ground next to her. Quickly, he grabbed it and searched for another water bottle, throwing things out of the bag until he found one. He gave the bottle a shake. It was full. As fast as he could, he popped off the top and threw water onto the sugar soldier. The soldier's head melted in a bubbly mess. Aunt Nellie climbed out from underneath the sparkling remains.

"Water melts them," Otto explained. "How many water bottles do you have?"

Aunt Nellie looked around at the field of commotion. "Not enough to fight them all."

"We have to find Droww," Otto said.

"Come on," Nellie replied. "I think he's over here."

Aunt Nellie grabbed her bag, and the two raced through the chaos as safely and quickly as they could. Finally they saw Colonel Droww and two of his soldiers surrounded by a group of sugar soldiers. Otto and Aunt Nellie grabbed her last two water bottles and sneaked up behind the enemy as carefully as they could. When they were in place, Otto opened his bottle and swung it like a sword. The flow of crystal clear water shot forward, striking two sugar soldiers. They screamed out in pain as they melted before Colonel Droww. Aunt Nellie took a big sip of water and sprayed the water out of her mouth onto the backs of the sparkling men. Within a moment, she had melted three more.

"Otto, my boy!" Colonel Droww exclaimed. "I'm so glad to see you alive!"

"I'm glad to see you, Colonel," Otto replied. "I figured out their weakness—they melt with water. But Nellie and I are all out. Do you have any?"

"I'm afraid not," Droww answered. "There's been a drought since the war started. Water is hard to come by."

"Colonel, we need water. It's the only way we can win this battle," Otto insisted.

Colonel Droww paused and looked out at the battlefield. Before him was a sea of sparkling sugar soldiers. Very few grasshoppers were left standing.

He looked down at Otto and said, "We've already lost this

battle, but with your discovery, I think we can win the war."

Droww ordered a full retreat. As fast as they could, everyone ran to the truck and climbed aboard. The colonel jumped behind the wheel. Otto and Aunt Nellie climbed in the front with him. The two remaining soldiers and fifteen grasshoppers piled into the back of the truck. They peeled away. The truck swerved in and out through the crowd of sugar soldiers. As they raced away, small sugar bubbles popped beneath the tires of truck.

Without warning, a sugar soldier jumped onto the hood of the truck. He pressed his face against the glass, trying to block the view so they would crash. Colonel Droww leaned his head out the window to see where he was going. Quickly, Otto flipped the switch for the windshield wipers. The sugar soldier cried out in pain as he melted away from the wiper fluid. He crumbled into sugar grains that blew away in the wind.

As they neared the edge of the battlefield, a line of sugar soldiers saw them coming. They stood arm in arm, blocking the

way. Colonel Droww slowed up on the gas, trying to figure out how to get through.

Seeing this, Otto reached his foot down and slammed on the gas. "Faster, not slower!" he yelled.

The truck lunged forward and accelerated. They sped faster and faster toward the wall of soldiers.

"Red Rover, Red Rover, send Otto right over!" he yelled as they burst through the chain of sugar soldiers. They all exploded in a sweet cloud.

The survivors from the battle continued racing through the Grasshopper Fields toward the Kingdom of Color. The farther north they went, the fewer sugar bubbles they saw coming out of the ground. By the time they reached Vegetable Valley, the sugar bubbles were gone completely.

"Are we going to get more water?" Otto asked.

"Not yet," Colonel Droww replied. "We need to go to the castle and let the generals know how to defeat the sugar soldiers."

chapter 10

The War Room

On a seemingly endless drive, the truck raced down the winding road toward the castle. Otto was anxious to meet the generals and didn't know what to expect. Would the generals be bright and helpful like Colonel Droww, or would they be stupid and set in their ways like the war inspector? Only time would tell.

Otto gazed onto the landscape of the Kingdom of Color. The fields on either side of the road were flowing waves of brownish gray. He wondered what it had looked like before the war, when the colors ran vibrant. From hearing the colonel talk about it, he imagined it must have been even more beautiful and rich with color than his own home. His mind then wandered to memories of his family. He wondered if he would survive the war. His head filled with fears that he might never get home.

Just as Otto's thoughts were about to consume him, the truck rounded over a hill and the Rainbow Castle of the Kingdom of Color came into view. It was a glorious sight. Brilliant colors illuminated the castle like a beacon in the sky. Even the land immediately surrounding the palace flowed with amazing colors. The castle walls were magnificent columns of alternating colors that almost looked like giant color crayons stacked in a row. Otto was in awe when he noticed that all along the wall was a street full of buildings and cars and people. It looked like a whole city standing on a giant pillar of color.

Colonel Droww stopped the truck at the bottom of a grand

staircase leading to the top of the castle walls. Soldiers in colorful camouflage stood guard at the bottom of the stairs. The grasshoppers and Droww's soldiers stayed with the truck while Droww, Otto, and Aunt Nellie climbed the stairs to meet the generals. Otto was delighted—as they stepped on each stair, it changed colors beneath their feet. Blue changed to red, green changed to pink, brown changed to yellow. It truly was an amazing and beautiful palace.

The three rushed through the crowds of people. Before Otto knew it, they were standing at a door guarded by four large soldiers.

As Colonel Droww stepped up, they saluted and shouted in unison, "Welcome back, son of Will the Great!"

Colonel Droww's face crumpled with frustration as he saluted back and entered. Otto and Nellie followed close behind. But before the two made it past the door, the guards grabbed them and threw them back into the street.

Otto looked up in shock. "What's your problem?" he shouted. "We're going with Colonel Droww to address the generals!"

One of the guards pointed at him. "Only officers in the Army of Color are allowed to speak with the generals. Take your grandma and go home."

"But sir, I'm Colonel Droww's personal assistant in all war matters," Otto explained. "He needs me as his council in addressing the generals."

"Only officers are allowed to enter," the guard retorted rudely. "*Officer* is spelled o-f-f, and *assistant* starts with *a*, so you cannot enter."

Otto paused for a moment, suddenly feeling as though he were talking to a kindergartener. "I have orders from Colonel Droww to stay by his side at all times," he tried.

"I don't care if you have orders from the king himself," the guard said. "No one is allowed to enter without officer stars on his or her arm."

Otto looked down at his uniform. It had no stars. Frustrated, Otto thought for a moment, then turned and whispered to Aunt Nellie, "Come with me. I have an idea."

After the two walked out of sight of the guards, Otto asked, "Do you have any fabric in your bag? And perhaps a needle and thread?"

"Sure do," she replied. "Why?"

"Because I'm about to be promoted," Otto stated.

Aunt Nellie handed him the supplies, and Otto quickly got to work. He used his knife to cut small stars out of Nellie's fabric and used the needle and thread to sew them onto the shoulder of his uniform. Within a few minutes, he was finished and ready.

"Stay here," he said. "I don't know if this will work, and I don't want you getting into trouble if it doesn't."

Aunt Nellie agreed. Otto took a deep breath, then made himself stand tall and confident. He walked around the corner and back to the guards. When he got to the door, he looked straight ahead and commanded, "Open the door."

The guards looked at Otto and quickly saluted. "Yes, sir, General, sir." They hurriedly opened the door for him.

Otto glanced back and forth at the guards. He didn't know quite what the stars meant or how many he needed. He was just glad his plan was working. Otto saluted the soldiers and quickly entered.

He hurried down a long dark hallway and into a large circular room. In the center of the room was an enormous round table.

Each chair around it was a different hue of the rainbow. Several officers were sitting on the chairs. The surface of the table was a giant map of the Kingdom of Color with little figurines spread across it, almost like a board game.

As soon as Otto spotted Colonel Droww, he rushed over to his side. "Did you tell them yet?" he asked.

"Shh," Droww whispered. "They are in a deep debate right now. I must wait to be addressed."

Otto stood quietly next to Colonel Droww and examined the room further. He noticed the bear with the hat sitting across the table giving Otto a scowl. Otto had not been formally introduced to Colonel Grivelt, but he couldn't forget his bad breath.

A name tag sat on the table before each general. Sitting closest to Otto was General Morgan, an old man with a wrinkly face and a sharp glint to his eye. Next to him was General Strong. As his name suggested, he was a muscular man with a flattop. Across the table was General Apa, a skinny younger man wearing a red bow tie with his uniform. Next was General Rock, a stern-looking man smoking on a long pipe. To his right was General Warbug, a round man with an enormous handlebar mustache. Finally, there was General Aldo, an old man with a tense look on his face. In his fist, he held tightly to a black whip. Otto feared he used it on anyone who argued with him.

"The time is imminent," General Aldo commanded. "This is a vital issue that we must decide before lunch."

"I agree completely!" shouted General Warbug.

"I don't think there's any room left for debate," General Morgan declared. "General Strong, General Rock, and I are all in agreement that this is the most prudent choice available to us. General Apa's objections have not amounted to a convincing counterargument."

"Not to you," General Apa burst in. "But I feel very strongly on the matter. I demand we discuss it further to explore every possible alternative."

Otto watched the fierce men debate. He had no idea what they were arguing about or which side anyone was on. By the serious tones of their voices, they must have already heard about the sugar people and were arguing the best way to defeat them.

"Enough!" General Aldo yelled. "The debate is over!"

A hush fell over the room.

"I have heard all the arguments," General Aldo said. "I have made my decision. The majority of you wise and experienced men are in agreement, but I must side with General Warbug's analysis. We will have chocolate ice cream with our lunch. Now let's move on to the next topic of discussion: What dessert will we have for dinner? General Strong, want do you think?"

Otto stared in disbelief. Did they just say ice cream? Were the mighty generals of the Army of Color really wasting their time debating over the dessert menu?

General Apa spoke up. "Well, seeing as my position of strawberry ice cream was not ratified for the lunch menu, I move that we have strawberry cheesecake for dinner."

As the debate rolled on, Otto was utterly shocked by the useless discussion. "Excuse me," he finally interrupted. "There are more pressing matters before us than the dessert menu! There is a growing army of sugar soldiers in the Grasshopper Fields planning an attack upon the Kingdom of Color. We must unite our army and gather all the water in the kingdom to defeat them!"

The room fell silent. Every head in the room slowly turned to focus on Otto.

"And who are you?" General Aldo demanded.

"I am Otto from beyond the sea," he declared proudly. "I saved Colonel Droww, and I have witnessed the creation of an army greater than anything I have seen. So we must act now!"

"You are not a general," General Aldo declared. "Guards, throw this boy out of here."

Several guards from the edges of the room surrounded Otto.

Quickly, Otto leaped onto the table. "General Aldo," Otto shouted, "you are an idiot!"

Everyone sat back in their chairs in amazement. These old men had spent so much time in this room debating the finer details of dessert that none of them had seen action such as this in many, many years.

"The Kingdom of Color is in great peril!" Otto continued. "The Kingdom of Shapes has created a new weapon—soldiers made out of sugar. First they lull you to sleep with their tempting sweetness. Then they convert you into a sugar soldier with a kiss of death. Every one of us they transform turns into another soldier for their ranks. By now, they have consumed most of the grasshoppers and transformed them into more sugar soldiers. It is only a matter of time before they attack us."

Otto paused as the men stared at him. "But there is hope," he continued. "I have found their weakness: water. Clean, plain water dissolves their wicked sweetness. You must act now.

Gather all the soldiers and men and women from the kingdom. Strengthen them with all the fresh fruits and vegetables you can. Load them up with all the water in the kingdom. Then attack the Kingdom of Shapes with all your might!"

As Otto gave his speech, the guards still surrounded the table, waiting to catch him. Then Otto noticed a different man emerge from the shadows. He was wearing a black cloak, hiding his face. He had long black sleeves with black gloves. Otto stood motionless as he saw the man raise a rifle.

Instantly, the crack of the shot echoed through the room. Otto could see a green ball hurling toward him, but he couldn't move. He was about to be hit and could do nothing to stop it.

With the force of a train, the swirling green ball stuck Otto in the chest. It hit so hard that it pushed him off the table. He crashed down onto the floor. An immense pain rushed through his entire body. Everything went black.

chapter 11

The Great Sugar Desert

Otto slowly opened his eyes to a gray room. He was lying on the cold stone floor in a small cell. He didn't know how long he'd been there, but it felt like hours.

When he sat up, he felt a pain in his chest. He lifted his shirt to reveal a giant purple bruise. Then he remembered he had been shot. He closed his eyes, thankful to be alive. The rifles here must only shoot balls of color rather than bullets like the guns back home. For once, Otto was glad he was in the Kingdom of Color.

Then Otto heard someone coming down the hallway toward him. He assumed it was a guard. Sluggishly, he made his way to the door to look out the little window. To his surprise, it wasn't a guard but Aunt Nellie.

"Aunt Nellie, is that you?" he asked.

"Yep," she replied.

"How did you get in here?"

"Oh, you'd be surprised what an old lady can do. Now, whatever did you do to get thrown in here?"

"I yelled at the generals," he explained. "They weren't listening to Colonel Droww, and they were ignoring the problem of the sugar soldiers. I'm afraid they're unwilling to listen to reason. The Kingdom of Color is doomed."

"Well, first, let's get you out of here."

"How?" Otto questioned.

"With these!" Aunt Nellie exclaimed as she held up a set of keys.

Otto belted out a laugh. Then he quickly stopped himself before the guards heard and got suspicious. Metal jingling resonated through the cell as Aunt Nellie fiddled with the keys. After a few moments, a deep clank rang out. The door opened.

"Quickly now," she said as they made their way down the hallway.

As they neared the exit, they passed two guards lying on the floor sound asleep. They were covered in the same glowing glitter as the grasshoppers.

"How did you—" Otto started.

"The sugar," she interrupted. "I had saved some of it in case we might need it. Turns out we did."

"You're the best, Aunt Nellie," Otto said. "I owe you."

"Well, you saved me from the sugar soldiers in the battle," she explained. "So now we're even."

"Okay," Otto said with a smile.

As discreetly as they could, they opened the door and walked out onto the street. They tried to blend in with the crowd in case any guards happened to see them. After a few minutes, they realized no one was following them. They were in the clear.

"What's your plan now, Otto?" Aunt Nellie inquired.

"I don't know. With the generals not listening, it's only a matter of time before the Kingdom of Color is invaded and overthrown. There's nothing I can do. I think it's time for me to sail out on my boat and continue searching for home."

No sooner had Otto said that than he spotted Colonel Droww through the crowd. The colonel was sitting alone at a table in a café eating a bowl of ice cream.

"Wait a minute!" Otto exclaimed. "There's Droww!"

The two quickly ran over and sat down with him. Droww's face was frozen in amazement in seeing Otto.

"Otto!" Droww blurted out. "It's great to see you. How did you ever get out?"

"The right friends," Otto stated as he glanced over at Nellie with a smile. "What are you doing here stuffing your face with ice cream?"

"Orders," the colonel explained. "I've been ordered to stay here with my remaining soldiers to guard the Kingdom of Color. Every other soldier in the army is now under the command of Colonel Grivelt and invading the Grasshopper Fields."

"What?" Otto exclaimed. "They listened to me?"

"I don't know," Droww continued. "The meeting continued after they took you out of the War Room. After five more hours, I was finally able to speak. I told them you were right about everything that had happened. Then they voted unanimously to send all the troops in the army to battle the sugar soldiers. But they said there was no water to spare, so they sent the troops out only with their swords and color rifles."

"No!" Otto cried out. "They'll get slaughtered."

"They punished me for taking you under my wing. They put Colonel Grivelt in charge. I just know that when he comes back, they'll make him a general."

"We have to help the troops," Otto declared. "We need to get them water."

"I can't," Droww stated. "My orders are to stay here."

"You have to," Otto pleaded. "If you don't, they'll fall—and the kingdom will fall with them."

Colonel Droww hung his head and sighed deeply. Otto knew he wasn't getting through to the colonel.

Otto thought for a moment, then said, "But don't you see? If you take the initiative and bring water to the battle, you'll be responsible for the victory. Then they'll have to make *you* a general. Everyone will call you the Great General Droww."

Colonel Droww perked up, and his eyes twinkled with glee. "Okay," he said. "Yes. But we have to move fast. You two get all the water balloons and squirt guns you can. Meet me at the entrance to the castle. I'll get the water."

In a flash, they each scrambled off to complete the tasks. Otto and Aunt Nellie raided the local toy stores and gathered as many supplies as they could. Within an hour, they were ready and waiting for Droww to return with the remaining soldiers and grasshoppers.

Suddenly, a deep noise rumbled around them. A gigantic tanker trunk rolled around the side of the castle. It was Colonel Droww. Otto and Nellie cheered as he screeched to a halt beside them. The soldiers and grasshoppers pulled up behind him in their truck.

"Are you ready, Otto?" Droww asked.

"Yes, sir, Colonel Droww," he replied. "Did you get enough water?"

"I think so. This is all the remaining water in the castle. I even drained every last drop from the moat. Now let's go!"

Otto and Nellie climbed in with Droww, and the soldiers followed in the other truck.

The excitement of battle was building up in Otto. He was scared yet confident. With all this water and their new weapons, they would be victorious. He just hoped Grivelt and his troops had not reached the sugar soldiers yet. Because if they had, they'd likely all be converted to sugar by the time they got there.

Otto's mind began to wander as they continued across the increasingly gray land. Then all at once, he remembered the man in black who shot him.

"Colonel Droww," Otto inquired, "who was that man in black who shot me?"

"That was Colonel House," Droww explained. "He is General Morgan's right-hand man. He has no subordinates below him. He's always on covert missions for the general. House was in the same class at the military academy as Grivelt and I, but he was always last in everything. Grivelt and I were surprised House even graduated. I don't even know how he became a colonel."

"Why is he in all black?" Otto continued. "That doesn't seem like someone in the Army of Color."

"Oh, that," Droww stated. "He's a chameleon. He can change his skin to any color to match his surroundings. But ever since the queen was killed, Colonel House has dressed entirely in black. I think it's some kind of mourning. He must have been really saddened by her death."

Pop! Otto was startled by the sound of a small sugar bubble popping beneath the tire of the truck. His heart began to race. They were now in the Grasshopper Fields and moments away from the battle.

As they rounded the next hill, they saw an enormous battle

reaching as far as they could see. The entire Army of Color was intermingled with the sugar soldiers.

Colonel Droww stepped on the gas and drove into the heart of the battle. He figured their only hope was to position the water in the center and work their way outward with their water weapons.

When they came to a stop, they rushed to battle. Otto jumped out with Aunt Nellie and manned the watering station. He filled the water balloons, and she filled the water guns. Colonel Droww, his remaining soldiers, and the remaining grasshoppers loaded up with weapons and ran into battle.

Three grasshoppers used a giant slingshot to hurl water balloons into the crowd. The balloons shattered upon impact, exploding into a watery mess. Whole groups of sugar soldiers melted with each impact. Other grasshoppers ran through the battle crowd, squirting each sugar soldier they passed in the face with their water guns.

The water was working! It was turning the tide of battle. Otto could see a ring around the trucks that was now clear of sugar soldiers. And the ring was growing like a ripple on a pond.

Colonel Droww made his way through the cluster of fighting with a squirt gun in one hand and his sword in another. He disintegrated one sugar soldier after another. As he worked his way farther from the truck, he saw Colonel Grivelt slashing the sugar soldiers with his mighty claws.

"Grrrrr! What are you doing here, Droww?" Grivelt shouted. "You're supposed to be at the castle!"

"I'm just saving the day, Grivelt!" Droww announced proudly. "Looks like I'll be made a general first. Too bad for you."

"Not if I have anything to say about!" Grivelt shouted back. "The king doesn't look too kindly at those who don't follow orders."

"He doesn't reward those who leave their fellow soldiers to drown at sea either," Droww replied.

Grivelt let out an enormous roar in anger and pounced upon a sugar soldier, biting off his head completely.

As Otto hurriedly filled up water balloons, something caught his eye. In the distance, there was a huge sugar bubble larger than anything he had seen before. And it was growing fast. It was now bigger than the entire castle.

When Colonel Droww came back to refill his water gun, Otto pointed at it and screamed, "Colonel Droww, look!"

Colonel Droww turned to the twinkling, expanding, sparkling sphere. It was starting to bulge and grow taller than it was wide. While all the other bubbles were perfect spheres, this one was expanding into an unfamiliar shape.

"I think we're in trouble, Colonel!" Otto exclaimed. "I think it's going to pop!"

In an instant, Droww knew Otto was right. The colossal bubble was moments from bursting. He had no idea what would happen when it did, but it couldn't be good. He turned to Otto with a defeated look on his face.

Otto thought quickly. "The water!" he yelled. "Get everyone you can into the water tank of the truck! It's our only hope!"

"Retreat to the truck!" Droww yelled as loudly as he could. "Get inside the tank!"

The grasshoppers and soldiers near them took heed and sprinted to the truck. Otto opened the hatch at the top and jumped into the water. Aunt Nellie followed behind him, followed by a stream of grasshoppers and soldiers.

Colonel Droww saw Grivelt and yelled to him, "Come on, Grivelt! We must retreat to the truck to survive!"

"Never!" Grivelt responded. "Run if you like, coward. I'm too busy defeating the enemy single-handedly."

Their positions seemed reversed now. Droww felt as though he were sailing away to safety while his fellow officer was at sea. Except Droww hadn't abandoned Grivelt. He had tried to save him, even though Grivelt was too stubborn to go.

So Colonel Droww ran with all his might to the truck and quickly scaled the ladder. Standing at the opening to the tank, Droww turned to look at the giant bubble one more time.

No sooner had he focused his eyes than it exploded in a brilliant white light. A mushroom of sparkling white sugar burst into the air. A wall of sugar rolled across the land, consuming everything in its path.

Droww dived into the tank just before it hit the truck. The impact sent the truck rolling end over end more times than anyone could count.

The truck finally crashed to a stop, but the water inside kept splashing back and forth for several minutes. Everyone's ears were ringing. It took ten minutes for Otto to regain his bearings. He crawled to the hatch, wiggled out of the sugar-covered truck, and scurried up the pile of sugar.

Otto's jaw dropped as he looked upon the land. Everything was covered in sugar. There were no more soldiers. There was no more grass. The Grasshopper Fields were gone. In its place was a vast sugar desert.

chapter 12

The Mighty Lion

Otto gazed far and wide across the Great Sugar Desert and could see no signs of life. He crawled back to the truck and yelled into the hatch, "Everyone okay?"

Moans echoed against the walls of the steel chamber, and voices rang out, "I'm okay." Slowly, everyone in the truck crawled out onto the soft, sugary ground.

"All right, soldiers. Line up," Colonel Droww ordered.

The battered men and grasshoppers made a neat row on top of the pile of sugar covering the truck. There were five soldiers from the Army of Color and eleven grasshoppers left.

"Is that everyone, Colonel?" Otto asked.

"I'm afraid so, Otto," he replied.

"Then this is what's left of the great Army of Color?" Otto asked. "How can we ever defeat the Kingdom of Shapes now?"

"Otto!" Aunt Nellie cried out. "I think we have another problem. Look at the water."

Otto rushed over to the hatch and peeked in. The water was gone. In the fury of the explosion, the truck had cracked and the water had slowly leaked. Now it was all gone.

"Is there any more water in the castle?" Otto asked.

"I'm afraid not. I took the last reserve for the battle," the colonel stated.

"Then we are the last hope," Otto declared. "Our only chance is to venture into the Kingdom of Shapes. Hopefully with our small numbers, we'll be able to sneak past the Army of Sugar and into the castle. Maybe if we can capture their king, we can win the war."

"There is one more hope," Aunt Nellie announced. "We could find the mighty lion and persuade him to join us."

"The who?" Otto inquired.

"He'd never fight," Colonel Droww stated. "He hates war more than you."

"Yes, but the sugar soldiers are different," she explained. "They aren't men—they're a plague. They consume and destroy everything in their path. Look what they did to the vibrant Grasshopper Fields. For many, many years, this was a fertile land that supported all the grasshoppers. It was so fertile that the Kingdom of Color and the Kingdom of Shapes went to war to control it. And now it's a desert. These eleven grasshoppers are all that are left of an entire population."

"You may be right," Droww conceded. "If he joins us, we could definitely use his strength."

"So who is this lion?" Otto asked again.

"The mighty lion is the protector of the Red Berry Forest," Aunt Nellie explained. "He's a gentle soul trapped in the body of a ferocious animal. He detests any person who would harm another. He uses his mighty roar to strike fear in the hearts of the wicked. Ever since his reign began, the Red Berry Forest has been a colorful lush paradise for all the woodland creatures."

"Do you know this lion?" Otto inquired.

"I know of him, but we have never met," she said.

"Okay, then it is settled," Otto declared. "We head north to the Red Berry Forest to find the mighty lion. Then we'll head south, straight into the heart of the Kingdom of Shapes."

With that, the group began their journey. As they walked, Otto wondered if they would even find the lion—and if they did, would he agree to join them? Aunt Nellie had been right about so many things, but part of him doubted that the lion could be convinced.

The walk seemed to go on forever. Otto had not realized how big the kingdom really was. After a while, they reached the edge of the Great Sugar Desert and entered Vegetable Valley. It felt good to be walking on solid ground again.

By late afternoon, they had finally made it to a road. Then they started to pick up some speed. When they passed a sign pointing to the Red Berry Forest, Otto felt relieved that they were getting close. He was starting to get tired, his stomach was growling, and he felt weak.

Then he noticed the grasshopper next to him pick up a rock and start nibbling on it. Another had found a pinecone and was crunching away. When Otto raised his hand to wipe the sweat from his brow, he noticed his hand was now a shade of gray. He was slowly losing his color.

"Colonel Droww," Otto said. "I think we need to stop and rest and eat some good food."

Droww agreed. The group stopped on the side of the road. The grasshoppers wandered around the grass, picking up anything they could and putting it in their mouths. Some were eating grass, others small twigs, and some just had handfuls of dirt.

"Don't you grasshoppers eat any real food?" Otto asked.

"Pickings are slim around here," one grasshopper replied.

"How about you, Aunt Nellie?" Otto inquired. "Do you have any good fruits or vegetables in your bag?"

Aunt Nellie took her bag off her shoulders, unstrapped the frame, and snapped together her chair. She then sat down and started digging through her bag.

"I sure do," she said. "I have some beets, some peaches, and some dehydrated strawberries."

"Thanks, Aunt Nellie," Otto said. "Okay, everyone—gather around. It's time to replenish our color with some quality food."

The group all sat together in a circle and shared the food. As Otto ate, he felt his strength coming back. He could see the color blooming in his skin and clothes.

After an hour of rest, the troop started back on the road again. By nightfall, they had reached the Red Berry Forest. The long shadows from the moonlight crisscrossed the road in creepy patterns. If it weren't for the tall trees on either side, they would have easily lost sight of the road and wandered off.

"Okay, everyone," Colonel Droww announced. "It's time to make camp for the night."

"But we have to keep going, Colonel," Otto stated. "We have to find the mighty lion as soon as possible."

"It's too dangerous at night," Droww explained. "We can't see where we're going, and we're more vulnerable to attack."

"But that's exactly why we must go now," Otto said. "The night is more dangerous, so it's more likely that the lion is lurking in the woods to protect travelers from the dangers of night."

"But we can't even see," Droww replied. "We're guaranteed to injure ourselves stumbling in the dark."

Otto thought for a second. "Aunt Nellie, you don't by chance have any flashlights, do you?"

Nellie took off her bag and searched through it again. After a moment, she pulled out a small flashlight. "I have one," she stated.

"Hmm. Not quite enough," Otto said.

Nellie dug a little deeper, then pulled out a handful of long candles. "But I do have these."

"Perfect!" Otto exclaimed. "Can I have the leftover cans from lunch?"

Nellie agreed but looked at him with an odd expression.

Otto took each of the metal cans and cut small holes on one side. He then lit one of the candles and gently placed it into the hole. The light from the flame now reflected in one direction.

He held the first one up proudly and explained, "A homemade candle flashlight. The can only allows light in one direction. It lights up what we want to see, but it doesn't blind us."

"Very clever," Colonel Droww said.

After a couple of minutes, Otto had finished making one for

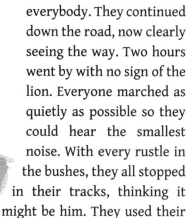

everybody. They continued down the road, now clearly seeing the way. Two hours went by with no sign of the lion. Everyone marched as quietly as possible so they could hear the smallest noise. With every rustle in the bushes, they all stopped in their tracks, thinking it might be him. They used their candle flashlights to illuminate the source of the noise, but each time, it was only a squirrel.

Otto was getting worried and impatient. It was a large forest, and the lion could be anywhere. Finally, he couldn't take it anymore.

He yelled out at the top of his lungs, "Mighty lion! Where are you? We are looking for you!"

"Why?" a voice whispered behind them.

Everyone spun around to see an enormous lion standing in the road behind them—only an arm's length from the grasshopper at the end of the line. The lion had a thick golden coat with a deep brown mane. Each of the lion's paws was as big as Otto's face. His shoulders stood taller than even Colonel Droww with his colossal head perched on top. It looked as though he could swallow any of them whole in one bite. All the grasshoppers fell to the ground in fear and scurried away from the lion.

Otto stepped forward and looked up at the lion. Otto was filled with fear but didn't want to show it. The lion could kill him in an instant if he wanted to, but he trusted Aunt Nellie's assertion that he was a gentle soul.

"It's a pleasure to meet you, mighty lion, sir," Otto said. "My name is Otto, and I come from beyond the sea. My friends and I have come here to ask for your help."

The mighty lion opened his mouth wide and yawned. His jaws were so big that Otto could have jumped right in.

"And what do you need my help with?" the lion replied.

"There's a new terror in the land," Otto explained. "The Kingdom of Shapes has created an army of sugar soldiers. Each wound they receive quickly heals itself. And they consume our soldiers and turn them into sugar soldiers. They are multiplying. It's only a matter of time before they invade the Kingdom of Color and consume it too."

The lion leaned his head down, pressed his nose up against Otto's chest, and sniffed him. "I am sure these soldiers told you I am against war," he stated. "And I do not participate in the adventures of the Army of Color."

"But this is different," Otto continued. "The sugar soldiers are like no force anyone has seen before."

"I am sure the grand Army of Color can handle anything thrown at them," the mighty lion reassured. "Go ask them to battle your ghosts for you."

"But they can't," Otto declared. "The entire Army of Color has been consumed by sugar. We are all that is left."

The mighty lion stared into Otto's eyes as if to determine whether he were telling the truth. Otto stared back at him firmly. After a moment, the lion looked at the whimpering grasshoppers and soldiers.

"Please, mighty lion," Otto pleaded. "We need your help. They have destroyed the Grasshopper Fields. All that is left is a sugar desert. Soon they will attack the Kingdom of Color. We are the only ones left to defend it."

"What?" the lion roared. "What did you say?"

"We are the only ones left," Otto repeated.

"No. About the Grasshopper Fields—what happened to them?" the lion clarified.

"They're gone," Otto stated plainly. "A giant sugar bubble exploded and buried the entire Grasshopper Fields in sugar. These eleven grasshoppers are all that remain."

The mighty lion roared ferociously, shaking the trees. "Okay, boy," the lion stated. "I will travel with you to the Grasshopper Fields. If what you say is true, I will join you and destroy each and every sugar soldier myself."

And with that, they set off on their journey—one officer, five soldiers, eleven grasshoppers, one old lady, one young boy, and one mighty lion.

chapter 13

Last of the Grasshoppers

Footstep after footstep, the group made its way south through the Kingdom of Color. Otto felt better now that they had the mighty lion with them. Without any more water, they needed every advantage to fight the sugar soldiers. The lion was so big and strong that he could probably destroy three sugar soldiers with one strike of his paw.

By the next morning, the group had reached the Great Sugar Desert. Upon seeing the endless horizon of sweet sugar, the mighty lion collapsed onto the ground and wept. Everyone looked at each other, not knowing what to say. It was strange seeing such a large ferocious creature crumbled on the ground crying.

Otto slowly tiptoed up to the lion and placed his arm around him. Gently, he rubbed his fur and said, "There, there, lion."

The mighty lion lifted his head and sucked in his nose with a sloppy, wet sound. "How could anyone destroy this rich, fertile land with such saccharine garbage?" he asked.

"I don't know," Otto replied. "That's why we need you. We need to defeat the Kingdom of Shapes before they do this to the Kingdom of Color. Are you with us?"

The lion pushed himself to his feet and let out an enormous roar. "I am at your command, Otto. I'll fight by your side until we destroy the foul beast that could cause so much waste."

With a forceful stride, the lion led the way into the white sands of sugar. Otto felt an uneasy tingle up his spine as he stepped onto the soft, sugary ground again. Every step farther south led him closer to the Kingdom of Shapes. Anticipation built in Otto's heart. He kept his eye on the horizon, expecting to see more sugar soldiers ready to strike. Otto just hoped they could make their way across the Great Sugar Desert before they were seen. There was no place to hide in the rolling hills of sparkling sugar. Walking across the granulated soil was so slow that Otto was convinced the enemy could outrun them in a chase.

As they were walking, Otto noticed the grasshopper next to him reach down, grab a handful of sugar, and shove it into his mouth.

"What are you doing?" Otto exclaimed.

Everyone stopped to look back at the commotion. The

grasshopper froze in his tracks with sugar dripping from his mouth. He looked back at Otto with puppy dog eyes.

"What?" he whimpered.

"I'm hungry."

"Have you been paying attention at all?" Otto questioned.

The grasshopper stared at Otto, not knowing what to say.

Suddenly, Otto realized this grasshopper was not the only one with that same look. Several of the other grasshoppers wiped sugar from the sides of their mouths and looked at Otto like children caught with their hands in the cookie jar. Then, before his eyes, those grasshoppers began to shine with a white sparkle throughout their bodies.

Realizing it was impossible to get them to understand, Otto turned to Colonel Droww. "Colonel, we need to get across the Great Sugar Desert as quickly as possible, before the grasshoppers eat any more sugar."

"We're going as fast as we can, Otto," Droww stated. "It's just too hard to move quickly in this soft sugar."

"Maybe I can help," the mighty lion suggested. "With my paws so big, I think I can move rapidly across this terrain. Maybe I can carry them to the Kingdom of Shapes."

"How many do you think you can carry?" Otto asked.

"Hmm," the lion thought aloud. "I could probably carry four, maybe five."

Otto thought for a moment too. He had no idea how far they were from the Kingdom of Shapes. It could be another day to two away. The lion would have to make three trips back and forth to get everyone across the desert. There was no way Otto would be able to keep the remaining grasshoppers from eating the sugar that long.

Suddenly, a new idea popped into Otto's head.

"Aunt Nellie, do you have any rope in your bag? And a blanket?"

"Yes and yes," she replied quickly.

"Great," Otto said. "I have an idea."

As quickly as he could, Otto set to work. He started by laying the blanket on the ground. He then took the rope and made a giant loop that lay along the edge of one side of the blanket. The rope was so long that he was able to loop it almost four times around. He then rolled the side of the blanket tightly around the rope to make a thick edge.

"Okay, everyone. Climb aboard," he ordered.

"What is it?" Droww inquired.

"It's a makeshift sled," Otto announced. "Hopefully, it will last until we reach the Kingdom of Shapes."

The mighty lion grabbed the rope and prepared to pull the others on the blanket. As everyone climbed on, Otto noticed the grasshoppers getting sleepy already. They were yawning and acting sluggish. He figured that if they slept, at least they wouldn't be able to eat any more sugar.

Once everyone was ready, the mighty lion leaped forward and raced across the land. Puffs of sugar exploded into the air, and the unstable sled bounced across the white sands. The wind rushed through Otto's hair. He felt a rush of exhilaration. The white slopes rushing past him reminded him of sliding down the hills at home during winter. He closed his eyes and was almost back home with his family. Only the sweet grains of sugar collecting on his face were different. Otto wiped his face, trying not to swallow any.

The mighty lion pulled the others on the blanket for three hours. Otto was amazed at his speed and stamina. As they bounded over the next hill, Otto saw the Kingdom of Shapes on the horizon—a dull gray rocky land without any color. Otto could see the border between the sparkling white sugar and crunchy gray land.

He knew they were close. He looked back at the grasshoppers sitting behind him. Their eyes were closed, and they were swaying slowly. Otto couldn't tell if they were about to fall asleep or throw up.

Then one of the grasshoppers lay back and rolled off the blanket. A cloud of sugar burst into the air around him as he rolled to a stop. Before Otto could react, another fell off, then another and another. Otto yelled for the mighty lion to stop, and they came to a halt. They had made it so close to border—they were almost out of the Great Sugar Desert.

Otto stood up and instinctively brushed the sugar dust off his uniform. Then he realized that the grasshoppers must have been consuming every grain of sugar dust that had blown on them during the ride. They sure were stubborn. He didn't understand why they couldn't listen to him about the sugar.

Frustrated, Otto walked over to the grasshoppers lying in the white sand. They had landed in a sparkling pile. Otto couldn't tell whose leg belonged to whom. He reached out and tried shaking them awake. He tried one leg, then an arm, then a shoulder. It was no luck—they were snoring away.

"I can't wake them!" Otto yelled back to the others.

As he turned to the grasshoppers again, he noticed something odd. They started to glow with even more shiny sparkles. It looked as though a sugar soldier were converting them all at once, but there wasn't a sugar soldier anywhere in sight. Otto slowly stepped back in fear.

Then before their eyes, the grasshoppers' color was entirely replaced with a twinkling white. The shape of each distinct limb melted into a solid blob. Before Otto could say a word, a long pillar of sugar shot into the air from where the bodies had been moments earlier. It was three times as tall as Otto and came to a dull point at the end. Otto's jaw dropped as the sugar pillar started flailing around in the air.

Otto turned to run away, but the sugar pillar swooped down

like a tentacle and wrapped around his ankle. In a heartbeat, Otto was in the air and hanging upside down above the blob of sugar.

"To arms!" Colonel Droww yelled, seeing the new threat.

All the soldiers drew their swords and charged. As they approached, four more tentacles sprang from the ground around the pile. In the center of the pile, a circular mouth opened wide to swallow Otto.

The mighty lion let out a giant roar, creating a ripple of vibrations across the surface of the sugar. Courageously, he leaped toward Otto, chomping down on the tentacle holding him. Otto and the lion landed on the other side of the sugar monster and rolled to safety.

The creature now had eight tentacles. It was holding two soldiers and a grasshopper in the air. Before Otto and the lion could act, the monster quickly swallowed one of the soldiers in its sweet, sandy jaws. The lion roared out and charged again.

Colonel Droww swung his sword at the tentacles. Each time he sliced through an end, it fell to the ground in a crumbly mess— but then two new tentacles grew back in its place.

The monster held one grasshopper up in the air. The grasshopper lit up with sparkles and was quickly converted into sugar and absorbed into the tentacle.

They were losing the battle.

Otto raced to Aunt Nellie. "Please say you have some water guns left in your bag," he pleaded.

"I'm sorry, Otto. They're all gone," she said.

Otto rubbed his brow in frustration. Then Nellie reached into her bag and pulled out the silver water bottle.

"But I did have time to fill this one bottle during the battle. It's the last one. Use it wisely."

"Run," Otto ordered. "If I don't make it, you have to get to safety." Otto turned and looked at the battle.

Colonel Droww was using all his skill with his blade to keep from being entangled. The mighty lion had three tentacles wrapped around him, but they were not strong enough to move him. Each time he clawed one away, another grabbed him.

Otto opened the lid to the water bottle. Confidently, he walked toward the beast and yelled, "Eat me, you sugar monster! I dare you!"

He stood firm as one tentacle lurched forward and wrapped around his waist. He held tightly to the water bottle to keep it from spilling as the tentacle lifted him into the air. His feet dangled in the air as the sugary arm carried him closer to the giant mouth.

Otto waited until he was just above the snapping jaws ready to swallow him, then he dumped the bottle's contents. The clear liquid splashed down into the monster's mouth, dissolving the long twinkling teeth. All the tentacles twitched for a moment, then went limp and crashed down onto the sand.

Everyone crawled back to their feet. Otto looked in the bottle. There was only a tiny bit of water left. The mighty lion shook his head violently from side to side, shaking all the sugar from his coat. Colonel Droww put his sword away and looked around. All the soldiers were gone, consumed by the sugar monster. There was only one grasshopper left.

Colonel Droww walked over and gave Otto a big hug. "Thanks for saving me again, Otto."

"You're welcome," he replied. "Now let's get moving before anything else happens."

The battle-weary travelers climbed aboard the mighty lion. He ran across the rest of the Great Sugar Desert. Within an hour, they stepped off the sugary soil and onto the gray rocky ground of shapes.

Otto announced, "We need to stop. The grasshopper is not well."

They all crawled down from the lion and looked at the last grasshopper. He was coated in the now-familiar sparkles. He was sluggish and not feeling well.

"Thanks, boy," he said. "I think I need to lie down for a bit."

"It's okay," Otto said. "We understand. You lie down and get comfortable. We'll wait here as long as you need to rest."

But Otto knew what was happening. He and the others exchanged sad, worried glances.

Otto helped the grasshopper find a comfortable rock to use as a pillow. He held his hand as his body slowly changed. Otto waited until the grasshopper fully transformed, then he poured the last splash of water onto his face. He was the last of all the grasshoppers. Now he was gone.

chapter 14

The Metropolis of Shapes

It felt strange to be traveling across the Kingdom of Shapes. Otto, Droww, and Aunt Nellie all rode the mighty lion as they ventured farther into the unknown. The land looked different, but at the same time, it was similar to the Kingdom of Color. The landscape was barren of plant life and covered with rocks of different shapes and sizes. Some were perfectly round, while others had four, five, and even six flat sides on them. Otto even saw a rock that looked like a miniature pyramid. If he didn't know any better, he'd swear someone had made them.

The sky was covered with the same thick cloudscape they'd seen over the Kingdom of Color and the Great Sugar Desert. Otto thought some giant factories with huge smokestacks must have been creating all the clouds to drain the water from the land. Everything in sight was a dull gray, and the four of them stood out like a sore thumb with their vibrant colors.

"So where is the king's castle?" Otto asked as they continued south.

"I don't know," Droww responded. "Nobody from the Kingdom of Color has actually stepped foot into the Kingdom of Shapes."

"What?" Otto blurted out. "You've been at war for all these years, and we are the first ones to invade the enemy territory?"

"Yep," the colonel clarified. "We've always stayed in the Grasshopper Fields or the sea."

"Don't you at least have a map?" Otto pressed.

"Nope," Colonel Droww said plainly.

Otto thought for a moment. How could that be? He remembered the huge map on the table in the War Room. He had even knocked over some of the figurines when he was standing on it. Then he realized that the giant map was not of the Kingdom of Shapes or even the Grasshopper Fields. It was only of the Kingdom of Color. He wondered why they would only have a map of the Kingdom of Color if they were at war with the Kingdom of Shapes and had bases all across the Grasshopper Fields. And why was most of the army spread across the Kingdom of Color when their enemy was so far to the south?

The mighty lion abruptly stopped in his tracks. "I think I found it," he said.

Off in the distance was a great city. There was a collection of towers of different shapes and sizes reaching into the sky. Horizontal bands wrapped like ribbons all around the city at several levels.

"Wow," Otto stated. "That's a big city. If King Rhombus isn't in there, we're sure to find someone who knows where he is. But we need to be careful. A city that big is bound to have lots of guards."

The group pressed on toward the great metropolis. Otto tried

to think of a plan. They didn't have the numbers to fight their way in. They would have to be sneaky and hopefully bypass any sugar soldiers without being noticed, especially because they didn't have any more water.

The closer they got to the city, the more it took shape. The architecture of the buildings was so much more impressive than anything back home. It looked as though the entire city were constructed with giant building blocks. Some buildings were giant rectangles, while others leaned to the side like massive parallelograms. He even saw tall triangular buildings and a huge arch with windows all along. Many of the buildings were connected together with long circular skyways. Each building was decorated with shaped patterns. The windows were oval and even star shaped. It truly was a wonder.

In the center of the city were three spiraling towers that reached higher than any building. On top was an enormous sphere covered in windows.

"Look, Droww." Otto pointed. "That must be the castle."

The mighty lion continued to inch nearer to the city. The closer they got, the slower and more careful he was. Around the entire city was a great wall made of interlocking rectangular blocks. They stopped behind a large angular boulder a short way from the gates. Otto got down off the lion and peered around the rock. The opening of the gate was a perfect pentagon, and the doors were wide open. There were no guards or people in sight.

"Something is not right," Otto declared. "They're in the middle of a long war, yet there are no guards to the city."

"Maybe it's a trap," Aunt Nellie suggested. "With our color, we could have been seen from across the horizon."

"Could be," Otto said. "But if they had seen us, why didn't they just send out a legion of sugar soldiers to grab us? Wait here a minute."

Otto crept out from behind the rock and scurried over to the gate. Carefully, he peeked into the city and looked around. There was no one in sight—just empty streets with overturned cars and oddly shaped rubble laying everywhere. It looked as though there had been a battle. *Did Colonel Grivelt somehow survive the sugar bomb and make it down here with some troops?* Otto wondered.

He quickly waved to the others to join him. As fast as they could, they darted into the city. The four walked down the center of the road through the great Metropolis of Shapes.

"What do you think happened here?" Otto inquired. "Do you think Grivelt survived?"

Colonel Droww looked all around for clues. There were scars on the walls and broken windows on the first few stories.

"I don't know," he replied. "Maybe the people in the Kingdom of Color heard of the atrocities in the Grasshopper Fields and stormed here in a mob."

As they rounded the next corner, they suddenly saw an entire legion of sugar soldiers at least two hundred strong—way more than Otto and his group could handle without any water. The soldiers were marching the other way, but they still spotted Otto's group.

"Quick, hide!" Otto shouted as the sugar soldiers turned and started running toward them.

The gang quickly ran back around the corner. The mighty lion led the way with his great speed. They scrambled into a building through a broken window. They ran down one corridor, then another. Right, left, right, right, then up two flights of stairs. They stopped in a little café and hid behind some overturned tables.

Otto carefully peered out over the table and watched through a window as the sugar soldiers spread out across the streets looking for them. It looked as though they were safe for now.

"Find your own spot to hide," a voice whispered. "This is mine."

Otto turned and looked around the café. "Who said that?" he asked the voice.

"Go away," the voice repeated. "They'll see you a mile away

with all your flamboyant color."

"Who is that? Why are you hiding?" Otto walked toward a counter. He thought the voice might be coming from behind it. Slowly he peeked around the corner.

Without warning, Otto felt the cold steel of a rifle pressed against his head. He slowly raised his hands in the air and backed up. The hiding man stepped out. He was a gray man wearing a uniform covered in star shapes. He was wearing a hat that looked like a rectangle. Otto knew in an instant that the man was a soldier in the Army of Shapes.

"I said find your own place to hide," the soldier stated firmly.

Suddenly, the soldier felt a hot breath on the back of his neck. He slowly turned to see the giant head of the mighty lion breathing down on him. In fear, he dropped his rifle and let out a high-pitched scream. He leaped back, stumbling onto the floor. The lion forcefully placed his paw on the man's chest, pinning him to the floor.

"You were saying?" Otto gleefully asked.

"Please, they'll find us," the soldier whimpered.

"Who?" Otto inquired.

"Your sugar soldiers," he replied.

"*Our* sugar soldiers?" Otto said, perplexed.

"Yes," the soldier repeated. "You are from the Kingdom of Color, aren't you? You're exploding with color."

"Hold on, lion," Otto ordered.

The lion took his paw off and let the man sit up.

"The sugar soldiers are from the Kingdom of Shapes," Otto said. "They are *your* new secret weapon."

"No, they're not," the soldier explained. "We were attacked by the vile sugar soldiers a few days ago. We thought it was a new weapon from the Kingdom of Color."

Otto carefully looked at the man. He could tell by the fear in his eyes that the soldier was telling the truth. It now made sense why there were no guards to the city.

Otto picked up the man's rifle and handed it back to him. "It looks like we now have a common enemy," Otto stated. "We have to work together to defeat them."

The soldier carefully took his weapon back, keeping an eye on Otto. As the man took hold of it, Otto noticed that it was a color rifle. "Where did you get a color rifle?" he asked.

"Color rifle?" the soldier asked. "This is my shape rifle. It shoots cubes, prisms, and cones."

"What?" Otto said. "Can I see?"

The soldier reluctantly handed it back, and Otto examined the weapon. It looked exactly like a color rifle. It even had the same three-triangle logo on handle. Otto opened the rifle and looked inside. Sure enough, it was loaded with gray shapes. He closed it up and handed it back.

"Strange," he said. "It looks just like the color rifles our army uses."

"What are you all doing in the Kingdom of Shapes?" the

soldier asked.

"We're here to capture King Rhombus and end the war," Colonel Droww answered.

Otto looked at Colonel Droww, then back at the soldier. "Well, that was our plan," he clarified. "But now I think we need to talk to the king. I think our kingdoms need to work together."

"Really?" the soldier said.

"I promise," Otto replied.

The soldier examined Otto for a moment, then said, "Okay. If you're serious, I can take you to the king. But only you—not your friends."

Otto glanced back to the others, considering the proposal.

"If you go alone, unarmed, to the king, it will show him you are serious about peace," the soldier explained.

Otto thought for a moment. He didn't know if he trusted the soldier. Maybe this was the trap he worried about. But why would the Army of Shapes go to such lengths when they could clearly overwhelm the four of them with force?

Otto then turned to Droww and commanded, "You three stay here and hide. I think this might be our only chance." He turned back to the soldier and continued, "Okay, I'm in. I'm ready to meet the king."

chapter 15

An Audience with King Rhombus

The soldier from the Kingdom of Shapes scurried down the hall from the café and up a flight of stairs. Otto followed closely behind him, hoping not to get lost. The two ran along the wall like little mice, stopping every now and then to listen for the sugar soldiers. They crossed one skyway after another, moving from building to building high above the streets. Each time they passed a window, Otto peered out onto the cityscape below. The streets were littered with twinkling sugar bubbles and crawling with the sparkling white enemy.

They got closer and closer to the palace in the center of the Metropolis of Shapes. The glass sphere at the top of the spiraling towers was higher than any building in the entire city. It almost reached up to the clouds. King Rhombus must have been able to see his entire kingdom from there. Otto thought it must have been a beautiful sight, but then he remembered that the Kingdom of Shapes was always dull and gray. How much better it would have looked if the land were bursting with a cornucopia of colors to decorate the magnificent shapes.

Otto kept a close eye on the shape soldier leading the way. When the soldier rounded the next corner, suddenly a sugar soldier tackled him. He crashed down to the floor with the formless opponent on top of him.

Otto stopped in his tracks, not knowing what to do. Before he could move, another sugar soldier came around the corner and jumped down on the shape soldier.

The shape soldier struggled, but he could not free himself from the two sparkling, faceless men. He turned and reached his free hand out to Otto for help, but as quick as a rabbit, Otto turned and ran.

The soldier had a sinking feeling, assuming Otto had abandoned him. He would have to try to free himself. Using all his strength, he swung his free hand at the sugar soldier's head. But it just slid off the slippery face, leaving behind a sparkling residue of sweet sugar on his hand.

Within a moment, the two sugar soldiers had subdued him completely. The twinkling face of the enemy pressed against his. The shape soldier knew this was the end. So much for the alliance with the Kingdom of Color.

All of a sudden, a splash of water hit him on the side of the face. He was shocked to feel the sugar soldier go limp, then melt into a pile of sticky goo on top of him. The soldier sat up and looked at Otto standing before him holding an empty water bottle in his hands.

"Are you all right?" Otto asked.

The shape soldier checked himself up and down. "I'm fine," he said. "You saved me. How did you do that?"

"Water," Otto explained. "It's their one weakness." Otto extended his hand and helped the soldier up.

"I'm just lucky I found this last water bottle in a store around the corner."

The two continued on their way, scurrying through the skyways to the palace. After running for a few more minutes, the soldier stopped at a wall decorated with large and small diamond shapes.

"Why did you stop?" Otto asked.

"We're here," the soldier replied.

Otto watched as the soldier grabbed a small diamond shape sticking out of the wall. He swiveled it open. It was a small keypad panel with a series of shaped buttons. There was a star, a circle, a pentagon, a square, and a triangle. As fast as he could, the soldier typed in the code. One of the large diamonds on the wall opened up to a secret door.

Behind the door were two more soldiers wearing uniforms covered in diamond patterns. They instantly pointed their shape rifles at Otto.

"Freeze!"

Otto quickly placed his hands up.

The other shape soldier stepped in and explained, "It's okay. I'm Commander Zircon from the Diamond Squad. This is an emissary of peace from the Kingdom of Color. He's unarmed and here to speak with the king to end the war."

The soldiers lowered their weapons but kept them pointing in Otto's direction as a precaution.

"Okay, quickly," one of them ordered, waving them inside.

They jumped through the door and quickly shut it before any sugar soldiers could see it.

The soldiers led Otto across another skyway and up a winding staircase. The walls were decorated with beautiful shapes of all sizes. Some were indented into the wall, while others protruded. Each door they went through was hidden in the maze of shapes. Without the soldiers guiding him, Otto would never have figured out how to get here.

All at once, they were standing in the throne room. Otto could see the king at the end of a long hallway. Above was a giant dome of glass. Otto could see the endless ceiling of clouds a few hundred feet up. The throne was a giant heart shape that came to a point at the bottom, where the king sat. It was amazing that it didn't fall over one way or the other.

Otto marched right up to the king with Commander Zircon at his side and the two other soldiers behind him.

King Rhombus was a round man with a short gray beard with different shapes trimmed into it. He was wearing a crown adorned with enormous gray jewels of different shapes.

"And who is this you bring before me?" the king demanded. "A prisoner from the Kingdom of Color, I presume."

"No," Otto stated confidently. "My name is Otto, and I come from a land beyond the sea. I'm here to end the war between the Kingdom of Color and the Kingdom of Shapes."

The king chuckled. "Ha. And why would the grand Kingdom of Shapes want to surrender to King Fabian? Your sugar soldiers have caused much damage, but we have many hiding places in the shapes of this great city. We have not yet begun to fight."

"The sugar soldiers are not from the Kingdom of Color," Otto explained. "They are a new enemy that threatens both kingdoms. I'm not here to demand your surrender. I'm here to purpose a truce and an alliance between the Kingdom of Color and the Kingdom of Shapes."

"It's true," Commander Zircon interjected. "This boy saved my life from a couple of sugar soldiers. He knows how to defeat them."

The king looked at his trusty soldier, then examined Otto carefully. "Okay," King Rhombus said. "Do tell."

"Water," Otto explained. "It dissolves the sugar soldiers into a sticky goo. Arm your soldiers with water balloons and water guns. The sugar soldiers won't stand a chance."

"Water?" King Rhombus repeated.

"Yes, water," Otto clarified.

"Perfect," King Rhombus continued with a frown. "Water is the one thing the Kingdom of Shapes is lacking now, thanks to King Fabian and his wicked ways!"

"What do you mean?" Otto inquired.

The king raised his hand and motioned to the clouds. "Just before the Kingdom of Color attacked us, this impenetrable cloud cover befell my kingdom. It hasn't rained since. The drought has prevented the crops of shapes from growing, and the water in the city is all but gone. I always knew King Fabian was a wicked soul. But to starve a whole kingdom of its water just to win a war is downright cruel."

"Do you think the Kingdom of Color created the clouds?"

Otto questioned.

"Of course," the king stated plainly. "They came just before they attacked us."

"What do you mean *attacked* you? Didn't you start the war?" Otto asked.

The king looked curiously at Otto. "I don't know how long you've been in the Kingdom of Color. Judging by all your color, I would guess a while now. But perhaps you don't know that the Kingdom of Color started the war against us by attacking our port. It is common knowledge."

"That's strange," Otto declared. "They told me you started the war by murdering Queen Lusita. They only went to war to avenge her death."

"What!" the king shouted. "Queen Lucy is dead?"

"Yes," Otto answered. "Four years ago."

King Rhombus put his head in his hands for a moment. Then he looked at Otto, holding back tears from his eyes.

"Queen Lucy was the pearl of the Kingdom of Color. She was a magnificent beauty whom even the people of the Kingdom of Shapes admired. We never would have killed her."

"Really?" Otto questioned.

"Really," King Rhombus replied. "We have always disagreed with the philosophy of color. Shapes are the true beauty of the world. But we are a peaceful people who only fight to defend ourselves."

"Well, if you didn't kill her, then I suspect it was the same unseen force behind the sugar soldiers," Otto announced.

"I bet you are right, Otto," the king said. "And to think all these years and lives lost over a mistake. And all the treasure spent fighting the wrong enemy."

Otto was just a boy. He didn't quite understand the ins and outs of conducting a war. All he knew about war was that people in two armies fought each other. Yet something about the king's statement sounded strange to him.

"King Rhombus," he asked, "what do you mean by treasure spent?"

"Shapes, of course," the king explained. "In order to fight, we must have weapons. My kingdom has used most of the glorious shapes in my treasure vault to buy weapons and supplies."

"You buy your weapons?" Otto inquired further.

"Shape rifles don't just grow on trees," King Rhombus said with a chuckle.

"Buy them from whom?" Otto asked.

"From the gnomes," he explained. "They live deep under the Shadow Mountains. They are the finest weapons manufacturers in all the lands. The weapons are expensive but finely crafted. Those weapons have protected us and kept the battles outside of our lands."

A spark of realization rushed through Otto's brain. "I'm not so sure about that, King Rhombus," he stated. "I think I now know the secret behind this mysterious puzzle."

chapter 16

Descending into Darkness

Colonel Droww stayed perched at the window, keeping a watch on the sugar soldiers in the streets below. The mighty lion quietly patrolled the hallways, ready to pounce on any enemies creeping by. Aunt Nellie kept hidden behind the counter.

It had been three hours since Otto had left. They were beginning to get worried. Droww feared maybe it had been a trick. Maybe Otto had been captured. Or maybe he and the shape soldier had been discovered by a regiment of sugar soldiers and converted into sweet, mindless warriors.

The sound of footsteps suddenly echoed through the mighty lion's keen ears. "Get ready, Colonel," he said. "Someone is coming."

The two took shelter behind an overturned table and readied themselves for battle.

"How many?" Droww asked.

The mighty lion paused to listen. "Seven," he stated. "No, eight."

The next few moments seemed to last for an eternity. Colonel Droww held his sword firmly, running through his strategy for attack in his mind.

"Almost here," the lion whispered.

They waited, hoping it would be Otto. But in the pits of their stomachs, they feared it might be more sugar soldiers. The footsteps were almost upon them, then Commander Zircon and seven shape soldiers abruptly came around the corner. Otto was not with them.

"Colonel Droww, are you still here?" Commander Zircon announced.

The mighty lion leaped out from behind the table, tackling two of the soldiers and pinning them to the ground with his paws. The others stumbled to the ground in fear.

"Where is Otto?" he roared.

"He's okay—he's okay," a soldier whimpered. "He's with King Rhombus. He sent us to get you."

The mighty lion breathed hot breath onto the men and threatened, "If anything happened to Otto, I will personally make you regret it." Once the lion was convinced that they were properly scared, he let them go.

"Please come with us quickly," Commander Zircon said. "Before the sugar soldiers find us."

Colonel Droww, the mighty lion, and Aunt Nellie set off with the shape soldiers. The group sneakily zigzagged through the hallways to the secret entrance to the palace. When they arrived, they were taken to a room where King Rhombus and Otto were sitting at a hexagon-shaped table.

"Otto!" Colonel Droww said. "Are you all right?"

"Yes," Otto replied. "I've made a truce with King Rhombus. The war between the Kingdom of Color and Kingdom of Shapes is over. We are joining forces to fight the Army of Sugar."

Colonel Droww smiled. "You amaze me more and more, Otto. Nice work. But if the sugar soldiers don't come from the Kingdom of Shapes, where do they come from?"

"I have an idea about that," Otto stated. "Can you tell me where the Kingdom of Color gets all its weapons? The color rifles, the color cannons, everything."

"From the gnomes," Colonel Droww answered plainly. "They're the best manufacturers in all the land."

"That's what I thought," Otto said. "Did you know the gnomes manufacture the weapons for the Kingdom of Shapes too?"

"No," Colonel Droww said. "But that makes sense now. The shape rifle was just like our color rifle. So what's your point?"

Otto smiled at Colonel Droww and continued, "If they make all the weapons for the Kingdom of Color and they make all the weapons for the Kingdom of Shapes, I think it's quite possible that they also make the sugar soldiers. Only, we don't know who controls the Army of Sugar. We need to go to the Shadow Mountains."

A realization shot through Colonel Droww like a bolt of lightning. Overwhelmed, he sat down at the table.

"Otto and I have made a plan," King Rhombus declared. "My soldiers can create a distraction on the west side of the city. Then you and Otto can hopefully sneak out to the east without being seen. To help you get there faster, you can take one of my sail cars. Commander Zircon will guide you."

Colonel Droww glanced over to Otto with a smile and gave him a thumbs-up. "Sounds like a plan," the colonel said.

King Rhombus led Otto, Colonel Droww, Aunt Nellie, and the mighty lion to the throne room, where they could see the entire metropolis. The king had ordered his soldiers to create the diversion, then Otto's group would be cleared to head east.

They all sat by the window waiting for the signal. They watched the tiny white sugar soldiers scurrying around the streets like little ants. Everyone was silent at the edge of their seats, waiting for the call to action. The clock slowly ticked along minute by minute. The waiting was painfully slow until suddenly it happened. The little white dots all rushed to the west side of the city in unison. It was weird to watch the silent wave rush across town. They didn't know how the shape soldiers had gotten the sugar soldiers' attention, but they could see it working.

"Now's your chance," King Rhombus announced. "Follow me."

He flipped a secret switch on the side of his throne. A circular trapdoor opened in the floor in front of the throne. Below it was an enormous slide.

"Quickly," he said.

The mighty lion looked over the little hole, wondering if he would fit. He crouched down and dipped his front paws in. Then he stretched out his neck and wiggled his head inside. The mighty lion slowly inched forward until he reached the tipping point, then his whole bodily slid down the hole. Otto then took the plunge, jumping in with both feet. Colonel Droww followed closely behind, with Aunt Nellie after him.

Everyone slid round and round and round. They were inside one of the spiral towers and quickly rushing toward the street. Otto leaned back and enjoyed the ride. He closed his eyes. For a moment, he was back home on the playground near his house, feeling the wind rush through his hair. But this was the longest slide Otto had ever been on. It took five winding minutes to reach the bottom.

Once they were on the street, they quickly climbed aboard

the sail car. The car was an angular, aerodynamic vehicle with two poles rising out of the front. Each pole had a triangle-shaped sail pulling the car forward. Everyone leaned back in their seats, and Commander Zircon launched the speed sail. A miniature explosion fired a giant trapezoid kite on a string high into the air. It instantly was caught in the wind and rocketed the car forward.

The crew raced across the gray rocky fields of the Kingdom of Shapes. The Shadow Mountains were far off on the horizon, but they were making good time. They traveled down the road as quickly as possible, passing fields of giant cube, cone, and sphere boulders.

Otto was glad they had made it out of the Metropolis of Shapes without any more encounters with the sugar soldiers. He hoped the journey to the gnomes would be without incident.

But he soon glanced behind and saw they were being followed by the sugar soldiers. They had commandeered six sail cars and were in hot pursuit. Each was being pulled by a different shaped kite. Otto didn't know how it was possible, but they were gaining on them.

"Hurry up, Commander!" Otto shouted. "They're on our tail!"

Zircon pulled on levers and pushed on pedals to try to speed up, but nothing was working. The sugar soldiers continued to gain. Otto kept looking back at the cars behind him, then forward to the mountains. There was no way they could make it before they would be caught.

"Quick!" Otto yelled. "Into the boulders! Maybe we can lose them in there."

Without a thought, Commander Zircon swerved to the right and into the fields of giant rocks. Each enormous boulder towered over the little car weaving in and out between them. They dipped to the right and inched past a huge trapazoid. Then they turned to the left and curved around a giant pentagonal prism.

The sugar soldiers followed them into the field and tried to keep up through the scattered terrain. Without warning, one of their cars smacked into the side of a boulder and exploded in a powdery mess. Another nipped a cylindrical rock and tipped on its side. It rolled end over end to a stop. But four sail cars were still on their tail and gaining through the obstacles.

"They're almost on us!" Otto shouted. "We're not going to make it!"

Otto looked ahead to see his options, but all he saw were more boulders.

Then an idea hit him.

"Commander, take a hard right after the next boulder and head south. We'll jump out and hide behind the boulder. Hopefully, they'll follow you."

Everyone prepared to jump. Commander Zircon slowed down as he approached a cube-shaped boulder. As he rounded the corner, they all jumped and rolled onto the ground. As soon as they landed, they scurried back to the boulder to hide. Commander Zircon then accelerated as fast as he could to the south. Otto took a deep breath, not sure if they'd ever see the commander again.

Otto stayed pressed against the rock, as still as possible. He watched the sail car race away. A trail of dust kicked up behind it and spread out into the air. He waited and waited, hoping to see the other cars in pursuit. Finally he spotted one. A second later, he saw the second and third cars following the commander.

A sinking feeling built up in Otto's gut when he didn't see the fourth. Where was it? Did it crash? Had the sugar soldiers seen them jump off? Were the soldiers waiting to ambush them? How long should they wait before they ran toward the mountains?

At last, Otto spotted the fourth remaining sail car continuing after the commander. They waited ten minutes, then climbed aboard the mighty lion. He ran off toward the mountains.

They made their way back to the road. Within two hours, they reached the mountains. The lion ran up the mountain trail as fast as he could to the entrance of the gnomes' domain. It was a simple mine tunnel constructed with wooden beams that opened in the mountainside.

They all got down off the lion and lit their homemade candle flashlights. Otto led the way as they entered the mine and descended into the darkness.

chapter 17

The Gnome Factory

A warm breeze blew through the narrow mine passageway as they carefully walked through the darkness. Otto led that way with his candle flashlight. Colonel Droww was close behind him, with Aunt Nellie and the mighty lion taking up the rear.

The walls were carved rock that seemed to run on endlessly into the mountain. As Otto placed his hand on the wall, he could feel a gentle vibration. The stone was cold to the touch, which was a sharp contrast to the warm air flowing through the passage. Running along the ground was a steel railway. It must have been used to carry loads of weapons to the surface or to carry supplies down into the dungeon.

The passageway slowly descended deeper and deeper. It began to curve to the left. Everything was quiet, but with each footstep, it felt as though they were approaching something big.

They walked for over an hour until they reached a small room. Steel boxes covered with giant rivets were neatly stacked along the walls. In the back was an elevator protected in a metal cage.

With no other way to go, Otto and his friends climbed into

the elevator and pressed the big red button to go down. The gears screeched and moaned as the little elevator shook its way deeper into an endless hole. Otto was worried that the racket would alert the gnomes to their arrival.

"They'll hear us coming," Otto declared.

Everyone looked around for a place to hide. The elevator was a small box with nowhere to go. The walls were a mesh of metal that let them see the carved rock fly past them as they dived deeper. The ceiling was the same cage and provided no cover even if they were able to get above it.

"Prepare for a battle, everyone," Otto ordered.

As they continued down, a low rumble began to build. The farther they went, the louder it became. After a ten-minute descent into the abyss, the elevator finally screeched to a halt in front of two rusty doors. A steaming wall of heat and sound pounded against their bodies as the doors pulled open, revealing an enormous cavern.

Otto slowly peeked out and saw no one around. As fast as he could, he scurried out and took cover behind some metal crates. The others followed close behind.

They were now sitting on a platform above a gigantic

factory floor. The rocky ceiling must have been higher than three buildings. The ceiling then curved down to the ground in a giant arch that ran off in both directions as far as he could see. In the center of the floor was a long channel of molten lava. It illuminated the whole cavern with a dim red light. Otto and the others no longer needed the candle flashlights and put them away in Aunt Nellie's bag.

The factory floor was decorated with giant steel gears and machinery that clunked away at a steady rhythm. Otto could see the little gnomes hard at work below him, assembling weapons of different kinds. It was hard to see exactly what the gnomes looked like. All Otto could tell was that they were short and stocky and dressed in dirty clothing.

Otto glanced at the box they were taking cover behind. He noticed the words *Color Rifles* stenciled on them.

"Look at this," Otto whispered. He carefully opened the lid and looked inside.

Just as it was labeled, the box was full with neatly stacked brand-new color rifles. Otto searched around more and saw more boxes on the other side of the elevator. As he had suspected, they were piled high with brand-new shape rifles. It was true: the gnomes were constructing weapons for both sides of the war.

Suddenly, the mighty lion stopped in his tracks. "I smell something," he whispered.

"What is it?" Otto replied.

"Sugar," he explained. "I smell sugar."

Otto took in a deep whiff and concentrated on his nose. All he could smell was smoke and metal. "Are you sure?" he questioned.

"Positive," the lion reassured. "This way."

The mighty lion tiptoed down the catwalk, hoping not to alert the gnomes working below them. Everyone followed as he led them down a set of metal stairs and into a hallway carved into the rock. They continued to turn down one hallway after another.

Otto began to worry that the lion hadn't smelled sugar in the factory after all. Maybe he just had some grains of sugar stuck in his nose from the Great Sugar Desert. And now they were getting lost in the catacombs.

But then they reached a medium-sized room filled with more metal crates. Otto examined them closely. They had no markings of any kind. When he tugged on the top of one crate, he couldn't get it to open.

"Can you help me, lion?" he whispered.

With his powerful claw, the mighty lion pulled at the top and ripped it off. But his strength was too great. The side of the crate separated too. It fell to the ground with a loud clang, and hundreds of tiny white balls spilled onto the floor. It reminded Otto of when he spilled his bucket of marbles back home.

Otto picked up one of the balls and examined it. It was soft, squishy, and sparkling like the sugar soldiers. Carefully, he held it to his nose to confirm his suspicions. They were sugar balls.

Colonel Droww held a few in his hand. "What are these? New weapons of the sugar soldiers? Maybe ammo for sugar rifles?"

Otto thought for a moment, then replied, "I don't know. Whatever they are, they aren't good. And they're proof that the gnomes are behind the sugar soldiers. Maybe they got tired of supplying weapons to both sides and decided to take over both kingdoms themselves."

Suddenly, they heard people shouting and footsteps coming their way.

"Someone is coming," Aunt Nellie stated. "Quick! Hide!"

As fast as they could, they scurried into the shadows behind the boxes.

Two gnomes ran into the room and discovered the mess on the floor. The gnomes were shorter than Otto, but they had thick arms, legs, necks, and faces. They even had thick fingers. Each of them had scruffy white beards covered in soot. They scrambled around trying to pick up the mess as quickly as they could.

Then a figure dressed all in black walked into the room. He snapped at the gnomes, "What are you doing? You'll damage the sugar bubbles. If they get the slightest imperfection, they won't grow when I plant them throughout the Kingdom of Color!"

Otto placed his hand over his mouth, trying desperately not to make a sound from the shock. He couldn't believe it. Colonel House was the one behind the sugar soldiers! But why? Was he trying to take over the kingdom for himself? Otto had to know.

As quietly as he could, he motioned to the lion and Colonel Droww. He stuck three fingers in the air . . . then two fingers . . . then one.

The three leaped out from behind the boxes. Otto tackled one gnome, and Droww tackled the other. The mighty lion pounced upon Colonel House with such force that it knocked off his hood.

As soon as the scuffle was over, Otto gazed upon Colonel House. Just as Droww had described, he was a chameleon with scaled skin, a ridged brow, and bulging beady eyes. His skin quickly tried to change to the dark gray of the dusty ground beneath him, but his face was too scarred from burns.

Colonel Droww's jaw dropped in shock. He rushed over to House, leaving his gnome unguarded. Using his sword, he ripped open House's shirt, revealing more burn scars all over his body.

"You were there," Droww declared with a stern voice.

"You always did choose the losing side, Droww," Colonel House said with a nervous smile.

The freed gnome scurried away down the hall.

Otto noticed it and glared at Droww in anger. "What are you doing, Droww? That gnome is getting away!"

But Droww didn't even look at Otto or the gnome. "You did it, didn't you?" Droww pressed House. "You started the fire. You murdered the queen."

Then a wave of realization hit Otto. Droww was right. Not only was Colonel House in command of the Army of Sugar plaguing both kingdoms but he was responsible for the death of Queen Lucy.

Droww lifted House and shoved him against the rocky wall.

Colonel House squeezed out a chuckle. "Looks like you've figured everything out."

Droww was overcome by anger. He held his sword up to Colonel House's throat. He wanted to kill him right then and there. But he needed to take him before the king so a just punishment could be served. It took all his strength to keep from acting on his primary instincts.

Otto looked at House. "Why did you kill the queen?" he asked.

Colonel House stared into Droww's eyes for a moment, taunting his captor. He then looked at Otto and replied plainly, "Orders."

"Orders from whom?" Otto asked.

"King Fabian, of course," he replied.

Droww's eyes lit up with fire. It was a lie. He raised his sword back to strike.

"Droww, no!" Otto said. He firmly placed his hand on Droww's arm. Otto then looked back at House. "Why would King Fabian order you to murder the queen?"

"To start the war," House explained. "King Fabian knew the entire kingdom would be up in arms if they thought the Kingdom of Shapes had murdered their queen. He knew they'd give up anything to go to war and make them pay."

"But why would anyone deliberately start a war?" Otto questioned.

"Don't be naive, boy," he stated. "All wars are deliberately started. Someone wants them. Someone always gains from them."

Otto now understood what Droww had said earlier about truth being the first casualty of war. Otto's eyes opened wide, and he blurted out, "The gnomes gain from both sides. No matter who wins or loses, they continue to sell thousands of weapons."

"Clever boy," House responded, licking his lips. "But like King Fabian, the gnomes are just a piece of the puzzle."

Before anyone could speak, a whole troop of sugar soldiers burst into the room, surrounding them. The gnome who had escaped had returned with reinforcements.

They were captured.

As Colonel Droww lowered his sword, Colonel House smiled. "As I said, Droww, you always pick the losing side."

chapter 18

A Secret Treasure

Sugar soldiers carried Otto and the others down a narrow, winding hallway. One soldier held firmly to each of Otto's arms, holding him so high that his feet barely touched the floor. The mighty lion was so big that eight soldiers had to carry him, two on each limb. And it took two sugar soldiers to carry Aunt Nellie's bag.

As they were dragged away, Otto wondered where they were going and why they hadn't been converted to sugar soldiers right then and there. Maybe he would get the chance to confront the vile King Fabian himself. Otto watched as Colonel House walked confidently in front of them. There was almost a spring in his step. Otto didn't know the history between House and Droww, but there were definitely unhealed wounds.

At the end of the hall, they reached a thick wooden door with giant metal latches. Through the door was the throne room for the king of the gnomes. It was a small room with a low ceiling. The lion bumped his head. A bright red carpet stretched out along the floor leading up to the yellow throne. The walls were the same dark-gray carved rock, but mounted shapes decorated them. Each shape was sloppily painted with a vibrant color.

There was a green oval, a brown square, a pink octagon, and a teal triangle.

Sitting on the throne was the king of the gnomes. He was short, even for a gnome. He wore a white fur coat with little red dots sprinkled throughout. On his head was a tall crown ornately decorated with colorful jewels that were almost as tall as he was.

The sugar soldiers threw the prisoners on the floor in front of the king and surrounded them.

Colonel House marched up to the king. "These spies from the Kingdom of Color were found in your factory," he announced.

The king looked up and down at Otto and his friends. "Who are you?" he shouted in an unexpectedly high-pitched, squeaky voice. "And what are you doing here?"

Otto tried his hardest not to laugh. Once he took a deep breath and composed himself, he said, "My name is Otto, and I'm from a land beyond the sea. We have come to find the source of the sugar soldiers and destroy it."

The king giggled. "I'm afraid there's no chance of that, boy. My sugar soldiers are the most highly effective fighting machines ever created. There is no way to stop them."

"There is one," Otto announced. "Water. And King Rhombus knows their weakness too. Soon his army will emerge from their hideouts among the shapes and vanquish your sugar soldiers."

"Not likely," the king replied. "There's almost no water left in all the lands. My master has made sure of that."

"Master?" Otto said. "So the lowly king of the gnomes is just another toady. Who holds your leash? King Fabian?"

"Silence!" the king shouted as he jumped to his feet. Otto was surprised that he wasn't any taller standing than he was sitting. "Never you mind. He will deal with you in due time."

"You're wrong, King," Otto replied. "I will defeat him after I defeat you."

The king squinted at Otto and sat back down in his chair. "You're bubbling with so much confidence for such a little boy," he said. "But you cannot defeat someone you can't even reach. And no one can climb high enough to reach the castle in the air."

"Even if you could fly to the sky, Otto," Colonel House interrupted, "you won't get the chance after I kill you."

"Not yet," the gnome king commanded. "We are to hold them alive for now. The master has other plans for these little troublemakers."

"But King," House pleaded, "Fabian wants them dead. The lion has been a thorn in his side for ages. And Droww is nothing but a shadow of his old man, Will the Great. And the boy's attitude is infectious. If he escapes, a cancer of independence could sweep across the land."

The gnome king looked at House and explained, "Well, Fabian doesn't make the rules, does he? He needs to follow orders like the rest of us."

Otto blinked in surprise. If Fabian wasn't the master, than who was?

"Then where do you suppose we put them?" Colonel House asked. "You don't exactly have a prison in this dungeon."

As the king thought for a moment, Otto glanced around the room. There were way too many soldiers to fight. Otto's group had no weapons or water. But he didn't want his end to come deep underground. He didn't want to be converted into a sweet sugar soldier—or worse yet, be thrown into a pool of molten lava.

"Throw them into my vault," the gnome king ordered.

"Your vault?" Colonel House questioned.

"Yes, my vault," he repeated. "There's no way they could break through its door. It's five feet thick and solid steel. And if you're lucky, House, they might just accidentally run out of air in there."

A wicked grin stretched across Colonel House's face. "Yes, sir," he replied.

The sugar soldiers hauled Otto and his friends away again. They marched down the stone passageways toward the gnome king's vault. The vault door was a perfect circle of smooth steal floating in the carved rock wall. It had twelve keyholes in a circle in the center.

Two gnomes set up a small ladder just below the keyholes. One gnome climbed up to reach them. The gnome used different keys on a chain around his neck to unlock the locks one after

another. A deep clicking sound chimed after each lock was released. When the last one was free, the giant door rolled to the side and disappeared into the wall.

Otto and his friends were thrown through the door and into the dark room.

Otto rolled over to look at Colonel House. "What will you do, House, when there's no one left to fight?"

"What do you think the sugar soldiers are for?" House replied. "People were getting weary of the war between the Kingdom of Color and the Kingdom of Shapes. They needed a new, more terrifying enemy to be afraid of—an enemy that could be lurking around any corner. One that people would do anything to stay safe from."

"But why?" Otto pleaded.

"Haven't you learned anything, boy? War is the health of the kingdom," Colonel House explained. "When there is peace, people think they can do whatever they want. They think they can make their own decisions. But during a war, people are consumed with their own fear and anger. They follow anything their leaders tell them. War is not about defeating an enemy. War is about controlling your own people."

Colonel House waved good-bye to Otto and Colonel Droww as the vault door rolled shut. The sound of the door closing reverberated through silence. The room was pitch black. Otto couldn't see his nose at the end of his face. He heard some scuffling beside him and was excited to see light from Aunt Nellie's flashlight. She pulled out the candle flashlights and lit them up.

The flickering light of the candles shone across the room. This room was different from the rest. It did not have smoothly carved rock walls and an arched ceiling. Instead, it was a natural cavern with jagged edges. Long stalactites and stalagmites emerged from the ceiling and floor. The room stretched on into the distance as far as Otto could see and was filled to the top with overflowing boxes and bags of color and shapes.

Otto opened a box and ran his fingers through a handful of powdered color. In a barrel was liquid color.

"Look, Droww," he said. "This looks like all the missing color from the land. Colonel House wants the war for power, but it looks like the gnomes are using it to fleece both kingdoms of their wealth. The Kingdom of Color gave the gnomes all this color in exchange for weapons. The Kingdom of Shapes did the same."

"What will we do now?" Droww asked.

Otto shone his light onto the solid steel door. "We're not getting out that way," he said. "We need to go deeper into the vault. Maybe there's another way out."

Carefully, Otto led the group farther into the cavern. There were so many boxes and piles of treasure that it was difficult to traverse the terrain. Boxes of shapes had busted open and spilled all over the floor. The group had to climb up mounds of powdered color to continue on their way.

Soon they reached a lake of liquid green with swirls of fuchsia. There was no way to walk around it. They tiptoed into the pool to see how deep it was. Luckily, it was only up to Otto's chest. Slowly, they waded their way through the lake.

As they walked, Otto began to wonder what else they would find in the vault. Would there be skeletons of other unlucky souls who had been locked inside? Or perhaps strange creatures from deep underground waiting to eat any people foolish enough to go for a stroll in their domain? At least Otto had Colonel Droww and the mighty lion at his side. They could fight off any danger they might encounter. That made Otto feel better.

Otto then noticed another pond of liquid color coming from up ahead. A strange light reflected off its surface. Otto didn't know what the light was, but he felt a surge of excitement build up inside him.

As they trudged through the pond, the water level slowly dropped as they inched closer to the source of the light. They could now see a red glow bouncing off the stalactites and ceiling as well.

Within a few minutes, they had emerged from the liquid color and were walking on the rocky ground again. Otto could see the edge of a cliff up ahead and light illuminating from below. Maybe more gnomes were working away below the cliff. Hopefully, they knew a way out.

When they reached the edge, they carefully peered over the rocky ledge to see a hundred-foot pit filled with a pool of molten lava. Otto frowned. The light hadn't been from gnomes. The glow was just from the liquid rock.

Otto then noticed a small ledge with another vault door across the lava-filled gorge—and there was a rickety rope bridge leading to it.

"Look! A way out!" Otto shouted with excitement.

They all ran to the bridge and examined it. It looked old and ready to fall apart at any moment. But it was their only chance.

"Okay," Otto ordered, "we should cross one at a time, just in case."

Otto was the first brave soul to step out onto the bridge. It gave a low-pitched creak as he put his full weight onto it. Otto's heart jumped into his throat. He thought it was about to give way! But they needed to escape, so he forced himself to move on.

With each step, the old rope bridge swayed a little from side to side. The air was filled with sprinkles of dust that must have been resting there quietly for ages. Step after terrifying step, Otto made it to the other side.

Colonel Droww, then Aunt Nellie, then the lion each followed behind him. They all made it across.

They looked at the vault door, trying to figure out how to open it. Just like the first vault door, it had a set of keyholes. Then Otto realized they were not looking at a door leading *out* of the vault. They were looking at a door leading *into* another vault within the main vault. Otto had no idea what could be so valuable that it would need so much security.

He pushed and pulled on the door to see if it would budge, but he had no luck. "Does anyone know how to pick a lock?" Otto asked.

They all shook their heads.

All at once, a small white light illuminated from the first lock. The deep clunking sound of the lock opening echoed through the chamber. The light disappeared, then reappeared in the second lock. It looked as if the vault door were magically opening itself. Otto didn't know whether to be thrilled or terrified. He stood frozen in his tracks as each lock unlatched and the door opened.

Otto stepped into the dark room and looked around with his flashlight. The walls were solid steel and made a perfect square. The room was empty aside from a small open crate in the middle. A light glowed from it.

Otto cautiously approached the crate and looked inside. Resting on a soft blanket were two infant girls glowing with a beautiful light.

Otto swiftly picked up one of the babies to make sure she was all right. Aunt Nellie quickly ran over and attended to the other girl. Otto held the little naked body gently against his chest. Her tender little hand reached out, and she wrapped her tiny fingers around Otto's thumb. She stared up at Otto with a soft smile.

"Who are they?" Otto whispered.

"I don't know," Aunt Nellie replied. "But they are special."

Otto smiled back at the beautiful angel in his arms. "Then I will call this one Gwendolyn . . . and that one is Sapphire."

chapter 19

Shining Towers of Hope

Otto stood at the entrance of the vault and held the tiny Gwendolyn tightly in his arms. He gazed at the flimsy rope bridge stretching across the gorge filled with steaming lava. The lava's glow cast strange shadows upon the cavern's jagged ceiling. This was no place for two tender babies.

"We have to get these girls out of here safely," Otto declared.

"How?" Colonel Droww asked, perplexed. "We can't even get ourselves out."

"I have an idea," Otto said. "The inner vault door opened, but we didn't do it. I think these girls did it somehow."

Colonel Droww glanced at the infant in Otto's arms and replied, "But they are just babies. How could they possibly open a vault door, especially from the inside?"

"I don't know, but there's something special about them. I think they have a powerful magic. We need to protect them," Otto answered.

After another glance at the babies, Droww smiled. "Agreed."

"Colonel, I need you to do something for me."

"Anything, Otto," he replied.

"We need a safer way to carry the girls. I saw some bags full of color across the bridge. Can you go empty out a few and bring them back here?"

Colonel Droww saluted Otto. "Yes, sir, General."

As Colonel Droww walked away, Otto looked down at the stars still on his uniform. In all the commotion, he had forgotten they were there.

The lava gave off a lot of heat. Otto wanted to take shelter inside the vault, but he was afraid the vault door might close again. Instead, he sat down on the ledge just outside the vault. He sat with his back to the steaming pit to try to protect Gwendolyn as much as possible. She didn't seem to notice the heat. She just stared into Otto's eyes and held on to his finger gently.

Within a couple of minutes, Droww came back with five empty canvas bags. They were exactly what Otto was looking for. He handed Gwendolyn off to Colonel Droww and got right to work. Using his pocketknife, he cut one of the bags into long strips of fabric. He then rolled each strip several times over to create thick straps. He continued by cutting two holes in the bottom of two other bags. With the needle and thread from Aunt Nellie's bag, he then sewed the straps to the modified bags. Within a few minutes, Otto had created two custom-fit baby carriers.

Colonel Droww carried Gwendolyn and Aunt Nellie carried Sapphire as they took turns carefully creeping across the bridge again. Then Otto scurried across, followed by the mighty lion. Otto felt relieved to be on solid ground again.

They continued on, wading through the lakes of color and climbing over piles of shapes. The journey seemed endless. With every pile of blue, Otto thought they were almost there. With every stack of orange, he thought the door must be on the other side. And just when Otto thought they would never get there, they finally reached the front of the long cavern.

Otto took the girls out of their carrying bags and held one in each arm.

"Gwendolyn, Sapphire—we need your help," Otto whispered. "You opened the vault door for us before. We need you to do it again."

Each girl stared at Otto with a playful smile. The soft white glow emanating from them lit the area so much that they didn't need their flashlights anymore.

"Please," Otto pleaded. "For me."

Gwendolyn and Sapphire each lifted a hand and placed them palm to palm. A bright light burst out from between their fingers. It was faint at first but soon exploded across the cave. Otto was blinded by it. He squinted as best he could while trying not to drop the girls. And then, as fast as the light was there, it was gone . . . and the vault door was open.

An immense feeling of relief rushed over Otto's body. They were finally free. He stepped out of the vault and into the narrow passageway. Looking at the tiny tunnel, he remembered they still needed to escape from the dungeon of the gnomes. And then they needed to figure out how to get into the castle in the air.

"Come on," Otto ordered. "It's time to get out of here."

They placed the girls back into their carriers and set off down the hallway to escape. The mighty lion took the lead in case they encountered any more sugar soldiers. He was the best at sneaking around and could claw through three soldiers with one blow. Colonel Droww and Aunt Nellie held the babies close to protect them and tried to hide as much of the glowing light as possible.

As Otto followed, he kept a close eye behind them. He felt powerless to the action unfolding in front of him. He could only hope the mighty lion remembered the way back to the elevator— and that he was quiet enough not to draw attention to them. His heart pounded loudly in his chest with each silent footstep.

They sneaked down one hallway after another until they reached the main floor. The gnomes were working away on the factory floor, so focused on their tasks that they didn't see them coming. The clamoring noise from the powerful machines echoed throughout the enormous room, masking any sounds they made sneaking up the stairs and to the elevator.

A loud *thunk* rang out as the elevator jerked up and began its long trip to the surface. Otto anxiously watched the carved rock walls race by as they neared the top. Visions of sugar soldiers waiting at the surface plagued him. Their escape had been so smooth so far that there must be trouble waiting for them at the top.

Otto nervously watched as the elevator doors squeaked open to reveal an empty room. They had made it. After a quick walk up the tracks, they exited the mine.

The warm daylight felt like heaven upon Otto's face. He was so glad to breathe fresh air again. After a short pause to enjoy their freedom, Otto and his friends hurried away from the mine entrance and hid behind some large rocks.

"We should stop for some good fruits and vegetables before we set out on our journey," Otto suggested.

Aunt Nellie took out some cans of pears and pineapple. Otto used his pocketknife to cut the fruit into the smallest pieces he could to feed Gwendolyn and Sapphire. The girls slurped up every ounce of the delicious fruit. They cooed with delightful sounds of happiness.

When they were done, they secured the girls, then they all climbed on top of the mighty lion. He sprinted off from the Shadow Mountains toward the Kingdom of Color.

The mighty lion raced down the slopes of the Shadow Mountains and into the fields of shaped boulders. After two hours of sprinting at top speeds, they reached the edges of the Great Sugar Desert. The lion didn't break his stride as he leaped onto the white sands of the desert. Small clouds of sugar puffed into the air as he ran. The lion's huge paws allowed him to keep almost the same pace as they traveled north. Otto was amazed at his stamina as he kept going and going and going. Before he knew it, they had run across the entire Great Sugar Desert and had crossed into Vegetable Valley.

They continued north into Vegetable Valley until Otto noticed little sugar bubbles popping up out of the ground as far as he could see. The lion stopped and let Otto down to investigate. He knelt down and felt a bubble. It was exactly the same as the night in the former Grasshopper Fields.

"It's happening again," Otto announced. "The sugar soldiers are beginning to invade. We are too late."

Aunt Nellie took out a blanket from her bag. She spread it out on a patch of ground with no sugar bubbles, then laid the girls down. The beautiful babies furrowed their brows, looking up at the sea of clouds above them.

"Otto, look," Aunt Nellie announced.

It was the first time Otto had seen any distress on their faces. "What's the matter with them?" he asked. "Do they need a change?"

"Nope, not a change," she said. "I don't know what's happening."

Lying on the blanket, Gwendolyn and Sapphire put their hands together again. Their hands started glowing with a soft light that quickly became blinding again.

Otto shielded his eyes with his arm. "What are they doing?"

The ground began to rumble beneath their feet. Otto tried to look around, but he couldn't see through the bright light. All of a sudden, the light was gone. Standing before them was a glimmering tower. It was smooth and white, and it stretched into the ceiling of clouds.

"Look!" Aunt Nellie exclaimed, pointing north.

On the horizon, in the direction of the Red Berry Forest, was another tower.

"Two towers?" Colonel Droww stated in amazement.

"Yes," Otto said. "One for each girl. They must be princesses, and these must be their castles."

Aunt Nellie replied, "I told you they were special."

"I know," Otto said. "And what's more, the towers reach the clouds. So now we have a way to the castle in the air."

chapter 20

The Castle in the Air

Across the grayish-brown fields in Vegetable Valley, Otto could see several bulging sugar bubbles just waiting to release their army of sparkling warriors. Time was running out before the enemy invasion. He just hoped they could reach the castle in the air and defeat the evil within before they ravaged the land.

Otto, Colonel Droww, and the mighty lion raced as fast as they could up the long spiral staircase through the center of the tower. Footstep after footstep after footstep they climbed, hoping to reach their goal in time. Otto felt a sharp burning in his thighs from ascending at top speed for so long. He wanted to slow down or stop. But the fear of the sugar soldiers conquering the Kingdom of Color and converting everyone to mindless sugar monsters pounded in his brain. Otto and his friends were the only chance. They couldn't give up because they were tired.

Aunt Nellie stayed behind watching the precious Gwendolyn and Sapphire. Otto thought their magic might be helpful in their battle, but he couldn't risk any harm coming to them. He didn't know what dangers lay ahead. Another legion of sugar soldiers could be waiting at the gates to the castle—or maybe something even worse. Otto was scared, but he felt good that they had made it this far. And with Colonel Droww and the mighty lion by his side, they could be victorious.

After a long while of running, Otto couldn't climb any higher. His legs just couldn't handle it. He stopped and sat down on the stairs for a rest. He glanced over the railing and down the curving staircase below. They were so far up that the bottom was unrecognizable. The spiraling lines seemed to spin closer and closer into a single point. He was amazed at how far they had come . . . until he glanced up and saw the same sight above. It looked as though they had a lifetime more to climb.

They took a brief rest, then Otto climbed onto the lion's back. They continued up the stairs. Another hour more, and they finally reached a small landing with an ornate little wooden door. Otto leaped off the lion and opened it.

Beyond was a grand bedroom decorated with pink and lace. In the center was a queen-sized bed with a dark-pink bedspread covered with a small mountain of red, purple, green, and blue pillows. Along the wall were an armoire, a table, and a beautiful cherrywood dresser. On another side, light-blue shelves were built into the wall. The shelves were covered with a plethora of dolls and stuffed animals. It was a little girl's dream.

Powerful sunlight beamed into the room through a large arched doorway. Beyond the doors was a small balcony, where Otto found the most amazing sight. Outstretching across the horizon as far as he could see was a gentle sea. The shining sun shimmered off the calm blue waters.

"Look!" Otto gasped. "An ocean! An ocean above the clouds!"

Droww and the lion rushed out onto the balcony to see with their own eyes. Their jaws dropped as they marveled at the endless waters.

Way off on the horizon was a castle floating in the pool of clouds. It was the castle in the air—where they needed to go.

"This is where all the water has gone!" Otto exclaimed. "It wasn't the Kingdom of Shapes or the Kingdom of Colors. It was the castle in the air preventing the clouds from raining."

"How deep do you think the water is?" Colonel Droww asked.

"Deep," Otto replied. "You said it hasn't rained since the war started four years ago. This is four years' worth of rain. We're going to need a boat."

Otto glanced around the room, but there was no boat to be found. The thought of the sugar soldiers bursting from their bubbles at any minute rattled in his brain. They didn't have time to travel all the way down the stairs to get a boat and carry it back up. Their only hope was to make one.

After examining the room, Otto started with the shelves. He cleared them off and disassembled them into wooden planks. He then found more wooden planks holding up the mattress under the bed. Within a few minutes, he had his idea. He would make a raft.

They set to work taking apart the furniture and collecting all the wood they could find. Otto used his pocketknife to cut the bedsheets into thin strips that he knotted together to make a rope.

Once they were ready, they assembled the planks in a single flat layer with several perpendicular boards as a support frame. They then used the homemade rope to latch the pieces together. Before they knew it, they had a solid raft floating in the water. Otto leaped off the balcony and splashed down into the still water. Bubbles swirled all around him as he quickly swam to the surface. The water was warm and refreshing. As he squirted the water from his mouth, he was excited that it was fresh. Otto always enjoyed sailing in the ocean, but he never liked the taste of saltwater in his mouth.

Colonel Droww and the mighty lion dived in after him, each creating a large disturbance in the water. Within a few minutes, they had crawled onto their raft and were off.

Using pieces of dresser drawers, they began paddling their way toward the castle. Otto had hoped to make a sail, but he had needed all the sheets for the homemade rope. Paddling was slow moving, but after an hour, they got into a good rhythm. The mighty lion was on one side, and Otto and Colonel Droww were on the other. They all placed their boards in the water at the same time and pushed together. With each stroke, the raft lurched forward, then slipped back a little when they raised their paddles from the water. The gyrating motion almost felt as though they were riding a horse. Luckily, Otto was used to sailing. He never got seasick, especially on such smooth, gentle waters.

Eventually, Otto noticed long waves starting to form. The raft began to rise and sink with each wave that passed. The tower was now so far behind them that he could barely see it sticking out of the sea.

His mind wandered to thoughts of the sugar soldiers running through the colorful castle in the kingdom below. Then a new thought popped into his head. Maybe they would run into even worse enemies at the castle in the air. Or maybe something terrible were swimming in the waves beneath their raft, waiting to eat them. He looked down into the clear water but could see nothing.

Then Otto looked up to see an enormous wave rolling toward them. "Hold on!" he yelled as it raced toward them. "We've got some waves ahead!"

They braced themselves as the huge wave hit them. Rushes of water rolled over the front of the raft as it started to rise. Otto paddled furiously to climb to the top of the wave. The swell was huge. It took them almost a minute to paddle to the crest. Once they reached the top, Otto could see an enormous gorge in front of them. The raft leaned over the edge, waiting to fall. It seemed they were perched on the edge for a lifetime, when suddenly the raft dived down the steep cliff of blue.

The raft raced down the mountain of water faster and faster. Otto stopped paddling and held tightly to the raft. His stomach dropped, overwhelmed with the sensation of falling. He feared they might dive underwater or tip over when they hit the bottom.

Then before he knew it, they splashed into the bottom and started back up the next fluid hill. Otto carved his paddle into the water and pulled with all his strength. Arm over arm, stroke after stroke, they pushed the raft up the next wave.

Otto and his friends continued wave after wave, paddling up and down. Each wave was bigger than the last, with higher climbs to the top and greater falls to the bottom. With each new crash, more and more water splashed over the front and onto the raft. Otto had dried off from his initial plunge into the water when jumping off the balcony, but now he was soaking wet again.

With the next crash against the bottom, Otto felt a shift in the raft. He looked down and saw gaps in the boards. The pressure of the water pounding against the raft was separating the boards and tearing it apart. Colonel Droww noticed it as well. He feared he might drown, after all. He dug his paddle in as hard as he could to reach the castle before their time ran out.

Over the next crest, Otto saw the edge of the castle and realized they were close. As he let out a sigh of relief, the rope in the center of the raft burst. The raft split in half.

"Quick! Over here!" Otto shouted to the lion.

The lion leaped off his half of the raft and into the water

behind the other half. His claws dug into the planks of wood in the back of the raft. Colonel Droww took the right side, and Otto took the left. They resumed paddling as fast as they could while the mighty lion kicked his hind legs in the water to help propel the raft even faster.

As they approached the castle, Otto didn't know how they could safely dock amid such enormous waves. The waves had grown so large that Otto couldn't judge the distance to the castle. He could see it only for a moment at the peak of each wave. However, the waves were also so strong now that Otto and his friends were entirely at its mercy. They were using all their effort just to keep moving forward and not tip over.

The top of the next wave smashed into the castle walls. On the next fall, the raft crashed over the wall. The raft exploded into many pieces, and Otto, Droww, and the lion tumbled onto a stone yard floor.

Otto sat up and held his head. He looked up and saw the giant arched door to the castle looming before them.

chapter 21

Invasion of the Sugar Soldiers

Aunt Nellie peered through the tower window at the growing numbers of sugar soldiers below. A glistening sugar bubble trembled as another sugar soldier emerged from the sparkling white wall. One after another poured out of the giant bubble. The attack was on.

The tower's double-door entry was locked tightly with thick steel bolts and a solid wood board. Gwendolyn and Sapphire were sleeping peacefully on a folded blanket on the floor. Aunt Nellie kept one eye on the twins and the other on the sugar soldiers spreading across the fields like locusts. She knew they were safe in the tower, but she remained vigilant just in case. Within a few minutes, the entire Kingdom of Color was crawling with the formless men.

In the Metropolis of Shapes, King Rhombus sat perched at the window of his throne room and watched the carnage in the streets below. New sugar bubbles had sprung up throughout the Kingdom of Shapes. So many sparkling warriors were crisscrossing through the streets that the dark-gray pavement looked like a flowing white stream. The light reflecting off the swarm of glimmering soldiers was so bright that King Rhombus had to shade his eyes.

Thanks to Otto, the king knew the key to defeating the wicked enemy. But unfortunately, the drought had dried up all the remaining water in his kingdom. He was the ruler of a mighty kingdom, yet he was powerless to the vile plague infecting his lands. He just hoped Otto was having success.

In the Kingdom of Color, six enormous sugar bubbles surrounded the Rainbow Castle, spewing out the unstoppable force. Legions of gooey soldiers marched up the rainbow stairs and through the street of the market. Colorful citizens ran in every direction looking for places to hide. They were no match for the overwhelming force of the Army of Sugar. Citizens were converted into more sugar soldiers in no time.

Hordes of sugar soldiers marched through every farm and village in the Kingdom of Color. They broke through doors and tipped over cars in their pursuit. Headless people—odd beings who called the Kingdom of Color their home—zigzagged down the street, bouncing off the sparkling obstacles. As the sugar soldiers encountered the headless people, they pushed them to the ground and marched on in search of their heads.

As the attack waged on, Otto, Colonel Droww, and the mighty lion stood before the castle in the air. It was a long, rectangular palace with many colorful columns running along its length. Each column was a different color, displaying every shade in the rainbow. Between the columns were spectacular stained glass windows stretching from the ground all the way to the top. The four columns in the center seemed to form their own larger building, which came out a good distance farther than the rest. Perched on top of a ledge over the entrance was a detailed statue of a black snake standing on end holding an eagle in its coils.

The fearless warriors climbed the short staircase before the entrance and opened the doors to the castle. Ahead of them was a grand room shadowed in darkness. From the light creeping through the door, they could see only a few steps in front of them. Otto wished he had remembered the flashlight he had left in Aunt Nellie's bag. He carefully stepped forward into the darkness, hoping he could find a candle or light somewhere.

The three brave souls spread out as they sneaked into the shadows. They proceeded slowly and stealthily, hoping not to arouse whoever held domain over the castle. As he crept forward, Otto heard a small sound like two hands rubbing together. He paused and held as silently as he could, listening hard to get a fix on the sound. He couldn't tell if it was Colonel Droww, the mighty lion, or someone else.

The doors to the palace abruptly slammed shut, reverberating a deep booming echo throughout the chamber. The room was now completely black. Otto could not see a thing. He held still, hoping his eyes would adjust, but there was no luck. He might as well have been back in the vault deep in the gnome factory without his flashlight.

Before he could act, a powerful force grabbed him. It wrapped around him like a thick rope. He could feel each band was twice as thick as his leg and more muscular. It wrapped several layers around him, starting at his feet and ending at his waist. He reached his hands down to push it off, but more coils wrapped around his arms. The skin of the strange beast was cold to the touch and covered with tiny ridges.

After a moment, Otto finally realized it was a snake larger than any he had ever seen before. Otto heard the muffled struggles of Colonel Droww and the mighty lion on either side of him. The snake must have been gigantic to hold all three of them in its coils at once. And it must have been incredibly strong to subdue the mighty lion.

"Guestsssssss," a raspy voice stated, breaking the silence. "It has been many years since I have had any guests. And to what do I owe the honor?"

"Let us go!" Otto shouted.

"Why?" the voice replied. "You are so nice and snug in my coilsssss."

Otto struggled to free himself, but the snake's grip was too great.

"Ansssssswer my question," the snake repeated. "Why are you here?"

"To end the war!" Otto exclaimed. "We know you are behind the sugar soldiers ravaging the land and stealing all the color and shapes from both kingdoms. We came to stop you and return the color and shapes to the land."

"What a brave little boy," the snake stated. "Brave, but ssssssstupid."

"Not as stupid as you think. I know you're the one who prevented the rains and dried up all the lands so no one would have any water to battle the sugar soldiers. I know you're the whispers in the ears of King Fabian that made him start the war between the kingdoms. You did it so your gnomes could collect every last bit of color and shape in exchange for weapons of war."

"Sssssounds as though you have everything figured out," the snake replied.

"Almost," Otto said. "I just don't know how you expect to get away with it. What makes you think the people will put up with it?"

The snake chuckled loudly. Otto could feel the moist breath blowing against his face. He couldn't see a thing in the darkness, but he knew the snake's head was right in front of him. He could hear its tongue slip in and out of its mouth as it spoke.

"The people are too busy with the distractions of war to realize all their color is disappearing. Sssssssoon they will be consumed with sugar. The people are too sssssstupid to realize I control every aspect of their lives. They are my sssslaves."

"But the war is over," Otto explained. "I have negotiated peace between King Fabian and King Rhombus. Soon they will unite their forces into an army even you can't stop."

"King Fabian is deep under my spell," the snake retorted. "Any treaty will not last. The king will use Colonel House to make sure of that. Nothing can stop me."

Otto managed to wiggle his right hand into his pocket and grab on to his pocketknife. As carefully as he could, he extended the large blade.

"Nothing but me!" he shouted.

He grasped the flittering forked tongue and held it tightly. Then he quickly swung his blade through the air, cutting off the tongue. As the snake rolled his head back and screeched in pain, Otto immediately stabbed his knife down into the flesh of the coils wrapped around him.

The snake's grip went limp. Otto scurried out of its clutches. He still couldn't see in the utter darkness, so he scrambled along the ground toward where he thought the door was. Instead, he ran into it with a thud and bump of his head.

Just as he reached up and grabbed the doorknob, the snake's tail wrapped around his left foot and tugged sharply. Otto clung to the doorknob as the snake lifted him into the air, pulling with all its might. It pulled, then pulled again, so hard that the door burst open. Light flooded the entrance. As beams of light struck the snake's tail, it burst into flames. It instantly released Otto and recoiled into the darkness.

A mighty roar exploded. The lion burst out of the shadows and into light by the doorway. Otto gave him a big hug. He was glad to see the lion had broken free. But that meant Colonel Droww was still in the snake's coils.

"The light! It's the light! The light is its weakness."

"How do we get the light in here?" the lion asked.

"The palace is covered in stained glass windows," Otto explained. "They must be painted black on the inside to prevent the light from coming in. All we need to do is break them. Now smash that door, lion!"

The mighty lion belted out a great roar. He tore through the wooden door as if it were paper. More light shone into the darkness of the room.

Otto quickly picked up a piece of the wood and threw it at the dark wall. It smacked against the wall with an echoing thud. He picked up another piece and threw it. This one smashed through one of the windows, creating a large hole. A sharp beam of light pierced through the darkness, illuminating more of the room. Otto threw piece after piece, shattering more and more holes through the windows. The lion ran along the wall, breaking the window bottoms with his claws.

A shaft of light carved through the shadows and fell onto the coil where the snake still held Colonel Droww. It burst into flames and released him.

Droww rolled to his feet and drew his sword. He quickly joined in the effort of smashing all the windows. As more and more windows broke, more and more light flooded into the room. The snake had fewer and fewer places to hide.

Soon the snake had nowhere to go. It coiled in the corner, howling in pain as the flames overtook its scaly skin. Otto watched as the snake squirmed wildly for a moment, then flopped to the ground. It burned to a pile of ashes. The snake was dead.

Otto cheered with joy. But the celebration was suddenly

interrupted with a violent shake. A huge crash boomed as a big chunk of the ceiling smashed down next to Otto. Then another fell down across the room. The castle was collapsing in on itself.

"We have to get out of here!" Otto shouted. "Now!"

All three rushed out as fast as they could. They whirled around and watched the columns tumble over into the courtyard. Then Otto realized the outer wall to the sea was crumbling as well.

"We have to get back to the tower before the castle sinks into the waters," Otto declared.

Otto and his friends grabbed the longest plank left over from the raft and jumped into the water. All three held on with their hands and kicked with their feet. The giant waves were gone. The water was calm again. Working together, they swam quickly through the gentle waves. Behind them, the castle in the air crumbled completely into the blue.

As they approached the tower, Otto realized the water level was lower than before. Not only had the castle in the air crumbled but the water was disappearing.

Across the Kingdom of Color and the Kingdom of Shapes, the ceiling of clouds finally released its bountiful waters. A heavy downpour streamed down for hours all through the land.

The millions of drops splashed down onto the Army of Sugar. The soldiers' sparkling skin bubbled and peeled off in layers. The sweet melting flesh poured onto the ground in piles of white grains. As the rains poured down throughout the kingdoms, the vast sparkling enemy dissolved into harmless goo that washed away in little puddles.

chapter 22

The Journey Home

The heavy rains poured down all night long. Otto took shelter in the tower with Colonel Droww, Aunt Nellie, the mighty lion, and the precious twins. He normally had a hard time sleeping with the sound of rain. But that night, he was so tired after swimming across the cloud sea that he fell right asleep. He awoke the next morning to a slight pitter-patter of the last drops from the clouds.

When Otto opened the doors and stepped out of the tower, he saw an amazing sight. The fields as far as he could see were shining with a vibrant green. Brilliant red tomatoes hung peacefully from thick green bushes. Succulent yellow corn peeked out of the ears of tall stalks. Long rows of purple cabbage, green lettuce, and orange pumpkins stretched off to the horizon. The sky was a soft baby blue without a cloud to be seen. A feeling of excitement burst through his body with the realization that the color had returned to the land.

After a long healthy breakfast of cantaloupe, strawberries, and carrots, they all set out for the castle to see the king. Using the homemade baby carriers, Aunt Nellie carried Gwendolyn, and Otto carried Sapphire. The girls sat quietly in their slings, watching the beautiful landscape with wide eyes.

As they walked along the road, Otto marveled at how colorful the land was. Purple, pink, and teal flowers lined the road in thick blankets. Blue birds and red butterflies frolicked playfully through the air. Happy squirrels scurried through the tall green grass, running here and there and everywhere. The bold, bright colors filled Otto with joy and excitement.

The closer they got to the castle, the more Otto thought about King Fabian. He was worried how he would react. Would Otto be treated as a hero for defeating the snake, or would he be thrown in prison for ending the war the king had started? Would the king still be filled with evil, or had the spell broken with the death of the gigantic serpent?

As they walked over the next hill, they could see the Rainbow Castle across the valley. It was decorated with the same cornucopia of colors as before, but it looked less spectacular sitting in a land now flowing with color. The marketplace was bustling with activity. People wearing flamboyant outfits of yellow, maroon, green, and blue scurried through the street with newfound fervor. Everyone was so busy running about that no one seemed to notice Otto and his friends marching down the street and up to the doors of the king's throne room.

The guards quickly led the group down the long hallway to

the king. The room was brightly colored with purple marbled floors and thick columns on either side of the red carpet. At the end was the golden throne that stretched all the way to the top of the vaulted ceiling.

Sitting atop the throne was King Fabian. He was a young plump man with rosy cheeks and a gentle smile.

"Congratulations, Colonel Droww," the king announced as they approached. "You have broken the spell and saved the kingdom single-handedly!"

"Thank you, Your Highness," Droww replied. "But it was Otto here who saved the day."

King Fabian looked down at Otto and smiled. "Then congratulations to you, Otto," he said. "I am forever in your debt."

Otto sighed with relief that the king was cheerful and pleasant. "You're welcome, Your Highness," he said. "But it was really the magic of the twins, Gwendolyn and Sapphire, that allowed us to confront the viper. They are as much to thank as the rest of us."

The king looked perplexed at the adorable infants. "These babies?" he asked.

"Yes, King Fabian," Otto replied. "They are very special girls. It was their magic that created the shimmering towers to the clouds."

"And where did you find these little darlings?"

"Deep in the mines under the Shadow Mountains," Otto explained. "We rescued them from the gnomes."

The king sat back and stroked his chin. His eyes carefully studied Otto and the girls. After a moment of pondering, he replied, "Then it is settled. Guards, sound the horns. I have an announcement to make!"

King Fabian rose from his throne and marched briskly up some stairs to a balcony overlooking the marketplace. Loud horns trumpeted out a royal tune, catching the attention of everyone on the street. The busy people stopped in their tracks and gathered under the balcony to listen.

"People of the Kingdom of Color," King Fabian announced. "It is with great pleasure that I welcome our saviors. These great warriors have defeated the Army of Sugar and saved us all."

The king motioned to Colonel Droww to come over. He placed his hand on Droww's shoulder and declared, "For your great service to the kingdom, I now bestow the rank of general on you." He turned to the crowd and continued, "General Droww is a great warrior and the youngest general in the history of the Kingdom of Color. And because the entire Army of Color has been destroyed, I am charging General Droww with the creation of two new powerful forces to protect the people: the Crimson Guards and the Royal Police Force."

The crowd all cheered for the new General Droww. He was overwhelmed with joy to feel finally acknowledged for his own accomplishments and no longer held under the memory of his father.

"The Crimson Guards," the king continued, "will be the most elite fighting force the kingdom has ever seen, sworn to protect the kingdom from all external threats. The Royal Police Force will be the safety patrol to protect citizens from all other dangers. They will patrol the streets of the kingdom and ensure that every person in the land is safe at all times."

The crowd cheered again. The king held his hands in the air to calm the crowd. When they settled, he stepped back and took Gwendolyn in his right arm and Sapphire in his left. He turned back to the crowd and held them up for all to see.

"And I have wonderful news to everyone in the kingdom!" he shouted. "These precious twins were rescued from the clutches of the evil gnomes within the Shadow Mountains. I have decided to adopt them and raise them as my own daughters. Behold the twin princesses, Gwendolyn and Sapphire. They will rule from the towers in the Red Berry Forest and Vegetable Valley. Their light will reign throughout the kingdom."

A thunderous roar of excitement exploded in the streets. The king smiled with pleasure. He stepped back to Otto, knelt down, and handed the girls back to him.

"That's the key to ruling a kingdom, my boy," he said with a wink. "Always tell the people what they need to hear."

Throughout the castle, a celebration erupted that continued for days. Otto felt great that he had saved the kingdom and restored the color to the land. But he missed his family terribly and knew he had to resume his search for home.

He gathered up a week's worth of food and water. He loaded up his sailboat that had been patiently waiting for him while he was on his adventure.

"Won't you stay?" General Droww asked as Otto readied his

sails. "The kingdom could use a clever boy like you."

"I'm sorry, General," he said. "As much as I love it here, this isn't my home. I need to get back to my family."

"But I need you," General Droww pleaded.

Otto stepped off his boat and gave Droww a big hug. "You are a general now," he explained. "Lead the people with honesty and fairness."

He gave Aunt Nellie, the mighty lion, and the twin girls each a hug. "Good-bye, my friends. Take good care of Princess Gwendolyn and Princess Sapphire for me."

Otto stepped onto his boat and pushed it away from the docks. He waved good-bye to his friends and slowly sailed away. They all watched as the little orange sailboat got smaller and smaller and finally disappeared beyond the horizon.

chapter 23

Book Report

After reading the last words of the book, Brandon closed the cover and sat in the quiet of the still tomb. It felt so great to know all about his Great-Great-Grandfather Otto and how he fought bravely in the Great Sugar War. A feeling of relief sat peacefully in his stomach. He now had his proof to vindicate him and Grandpa Alvin. Now it was time for him to escape this dungeon and confront Miss Carter.

Brandon looked up through the holes. It was almost dark. He was tired. He decided to get some rest before starting the long walk home. He carefully removed the blanket from the bed and curled up on the floor for the night.

The next morning, Brandon awoke with a brisk vigor. He got up and examined the holes in the ceiling for the best way to get out. The ceiling was more than twice his height. There was no way he could jump that high.

He scoured the room and hallway, looking for anything he could stand on to reach the ledge. But after a few minutes, he realized there was no ladder or rope or anything that could help. He sat back down on the floor thinking.

Then he remembered something he read in the book. Brandon leaped to his feet and began tearing down the green curtains hanging around the bed. He pulled out his pocketknife and began cutting long, thin strips. Once he had a good pile, he

took the fabric and tied them together with a
series of knots. It took a good hour of work. But
by the end, Brandon had made a solid rope. Once
he was ready, he made a loop at the end with a
slipknot. He stood under the largest hole.

Brandon swung the rope around and around,
then launched it into the air. It landed
out of sight through the hole in
the ceiling. He gently pulled on
it until it caught on something
up above. Then he pulled it
tight. Carefully, he hung from
the rope to make sure it could
support his weight.

When he was confident
that the rope was ready,
he laid a small rectangular
piece of green fabric out on
the floor. He placed the book
and General Droww's medals in
the center of the fabric. Brandon folded
the fabric around everything, then tightly
twisted the ends of each side. He hoisted the
bundle onto his back, wrapping the ends of
the fabric around his body and tying them
into a knot. It wasn't as sturdy as his school
backpack, but it worked well in a pinch.

Hand over hand, Brandon climbed up the
rope. It was a lot farther than he had thought.
By the end, his hands were aching with pain, but
it was his only way out. He struggled through it.

He reached the top, crawling out of the
hole and through the rubble. It took another
twenty minutes to cut his way through the giant

rosebushes. But soon Brandon was clear and running back to school.

As he ran through the empty fields, he wondered how his teacher would react. Would he even have a chance to explain about the book, or would he be thrown right into detention by Officer Reed? Brandon knew he'd have to sneak his way back to class. If he were caught beforehand, he'd have no chance to plead his case.

Without warning, Brandon fell down as the ground opened up. His foot was caught in a deep hole. Luckily, the hole was no bigger than his foot, which prevented him from disappearing into it completely. He pulled his foot out and stopped to look into the hole. It was pure black and seemed to sink deeper than he could see. Brandon picked up a small rock and dropped it in. He waited to hear it clunk against the bottom, but after waiting a whole minute, he couldn't hear anything.

Brandon looked back at the towering rosebushes off in the distance. He was a long way away. It amazed him that the Color Factory could have been so big as to leave crumbling holes this far away from its center.

But he didn't have time to waste. He rose to his feet and continued running across the fields toward his hometown. It took a couple of more hours, but soon he reached the edge of town.

As fast as he could, Brandon scurried through the neighborhood backyards. When he reached the school, he could hear the piercing bell ringing across the playground. Lunch was over, and kids were heading back to class.

In the commotion of kids running up and down the hallways, Brandon easily sneaked into his class. He confidently walked into the class and up to Miss Carter's desk.

Her eyes grew wide seeing him standing before him. "Brandon," she stammered. "What are you doing here?"

"You didn't believe me," he announced. "I told you the snakes created the Great Grayness and that my grandfather rescued the princesses from the Color Factory and defeated the vile vipers. But now I've brought you proof."

Brandon slammed the thick book down on her desk. The deep thud echoed through the classroom and got everyone's attention. The class sat silently, waiting for the inevitable fireworks from their teacher.

Quietly, she turned the book toward her, opened the cover, and examined it.

Brandon pointed to it and explained, "There, on the side cover, is a note written by General Droww himself. It explains how my grandfather visited him in the Color Factory. It's proof that what I told you is the truth and that the school textbooks are filled with lies."

Miss Carter closed the book, looked at Brandon, and said firmly, "This doesn't prove anything. You could have found this storybook and written the note yourself."

Brandon smiled and replied, "I thought you'd say that. But could I make official war medals from the king?" He pulled out General Droww's medals and held them in the air. "I found the Color Factory ruins, and inside were the remains of General Droww. These are the medals from his chest—official awards from King Fabian himself."

A dull murmur rolled through the classroom. Brandon knew he had convinced them of the truth, and so did Miss Carter.

She instantly grabbed his wrist and shouted, "Enough of your lies and stories! It is off to prison for you!"

She jumped to her feet and marched out of the room, dragging Brandon behind her. He was no match for her strong grip and could only follow down the hall behind her.

Once in the hallway, she stopped to scold him some more. Brandon knew he had come up with a plan, so he started his best fake cry.

"Please, Miss Carter—my mother's gonna be so sad if I go to prison," he sniffled.

As Brandon covered his face with his hands, Miss Carter released her grip to let him regain his composure. Giving the performance of his life, he waited until she glanced away. Then he made his move.

Quickly, Brandon raced back into the classroom and grabbed the book. Without stopping, he ran to an open window and dived out. He rolled to his feet and sprinted toward his grandfather's house.

He raced through the backyards again, dodging in and out between the trees and fences. Within a few minutes, he had reached his grandfather's door. He glanced back to see no one following him. But he didn't want to take any chances by lingering around, so he let himself in.

"Grandpa Alvin! Grandpa Alvin!" he shouted.

There was no answer. Where could his grandfather be? He was gone again, and it was not like him.

Brandon ran through the house, checking every nook and cranny for his grandfather. He couldn't find him anywhere. Everything in the house looked just as he had left it the day before.

Brandon ran down the stairs to the basement, hoping to find him in the last room left in the house. He had no such luck.

There was only an empty basement with shelves stacked with canned foods and an old table cluttered with tools. The floor had maroon-and-black checkered tiles. A tarp was spread across the center of the floor.

"Where could he be?" Brandon wondered aloud.

Brandon didn't know what to do. He was in deep trouble. He needed his grandfather's help, but he was nowhere to be found! Brandon clenched his fists.

Standing next to the table, Brandon suddenly picked up a screwdriver and threw it across the room in frustration. It bounced off the far wall, then skipped back across the floor, landing in the middle of the tarp.

Suddenly, the center of the tarp began to sink beneath the screwdriver. Brandon's eyes grew wide as he watched the tarp give away and disappear into a giant hole in the floor.

The enormous pit had been dug into the tile. It must have been big enough to swallow a car whole. Brandon stepped forward and peered into the deep. All he could see was darkness.

Instantly, Brandon knew why he couldn't find his grandfather. Grandpa Alvin had disappeared into the mysterious hole in the ground. Now Brandon was all on his own.

About the Author

My name is Benjamin, and I love writing whimsical adventures for children of all ages.

Childhood was a magical time for me. I grew up in a neighborhood full of kids. Every day was filled with imagination, adventures, fantasy, and wonderful stories. In school I loved any project that let me explore my creativity.

When I was older, I traveled across the country to study storytelling at the University of Southern California in their school of Cinema/Television. While in school, I had the amazing opportunity to work on several film productions and saw stories coming to life firsthand.

Over several years after school, I had four beautiful daughters. When they were little, I spent all of my creative energy giving them the magical childhood I had when I was small. There was nothing as exciting as watching their imaginations flourish as they explored the world.

Now that they are older, I want to give that magic to all of the children of the world. I focus my writing on modern fairy tales that are fun for kids and thought provoking for adults. Each adventure celebrates important values of self-reliance, preparedness, and diversity. I am hoping each book sparks imagination in readers.

www.benjaminellefson.com

About the Illustrator

Kevin Cannon is a cartoonist most well known for the critically acclaimed nonfiction graphic novel *The Cartoon Introduction to Philosophy* (Hill & Wang, 2015) and the Eisner Award-nominated arctic adventure *Far Arden* (Top Shelf, 2009). *City Pages* named him Twin Cities' Best Cartoonist in 2011. He also produces elaborate cartoon maps, which have appeared in *The Appendix*, *The Star Tribune*, *The Riverfront Times*, and *The Miami New Times*.

Cannon has also illustrated several children's books, most notably *Ben and Lucy Play Pond Hockey* (Beavers Pond Press, 2010), and *The Adventures of Team Super Tubie* (Beavers Pond Press, 2017).

A Minneapolis native, Cannon spends his free time camping, reading dusty books about arctic explorers, and listening to hockey games on the radio.

www.kevincannon.org

The adventure concludes in the next book...

www.benjaminellefson.com/Collapsing-Kingdom